UK Geography Activity Book for Kids

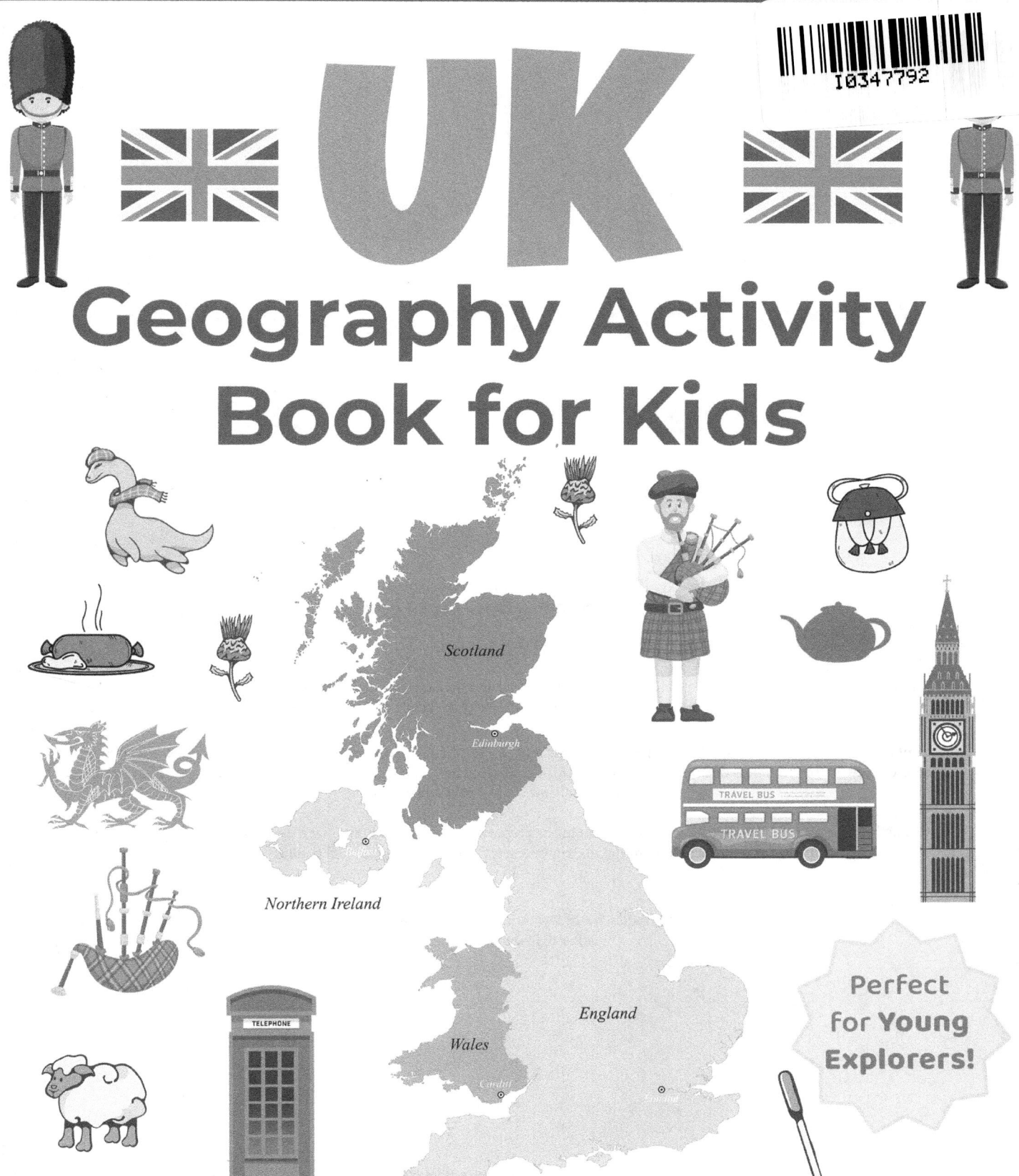

Perfect for Young Explorers!

Fun Facts, Puzzles, Maps, Legends, and More
Learn About England, Scotland, Wales, and Northern Ireland!

Published by Dylanna Press an imprint of Dylanna Publishing, Inc.
Copyright © 2025 by Dylanna Press

Editor: Julie Grady

All rights reserved. No part of this publication may be reproduced, stored in a retrieval system, or transmitted by any means, including electronic, mechanical, photocopying, or otherwise, without prior written permission of the publisher.

Limit of liability/Disclaimer of Warranty: The Publisher and the author make no representations or warranties with respect to the accuracy or completeness of the contents of this work and specifically disclaim all warranties, including without limitation warranties of fitness for a particular purpose.

Although the publisher has taken all reasonable care in the preparation of this book, we make no warranty about the accuracy or completeness of its content and, to the maximum extent permitted, disclaim all liability arising from its use.

Trademarks: Dylanna Press is a registered trademark of Dylanna Publishing, Inc. and may not be used without written permission.
info@dylannapubishing.com

WELCOME TO THE UNITED KINGDOM!

Get ready for an exciting journey through one of the most fascinating places in the world—the United Kingdom, or the UK for short! This book is packed with fun facts, cool activities, and amazing discoveries that will help you learn all about this group of countries filled with castles, legends, landmarks, and traditions.

The UK is made up of four nations:

- England
- Scotland
- Wales
- Northern Ireland

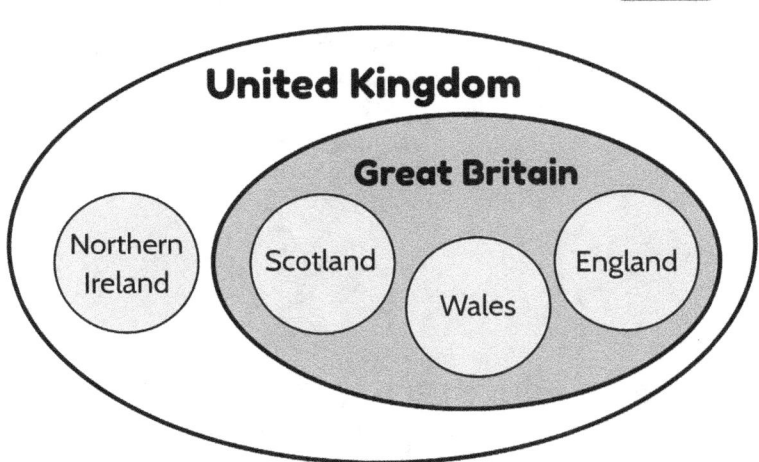

In this book, you'll:

- Explore famous cities, natural wonders, and historical sites
- Learn about kings and queens, inventors, writers, and world-changing events
- Discover what people eat, how they celebrate, and even how they speak differently across the United Kingdom
- Play games, solve puzzles, color cool pictures, and read stories!

Whether you're visiting from afar or learning from home, you're about to uncover what makes the UK unique, proud, and full of personality.

So grab your pencil—and maybe a scone or two—and let's start our adventure!

Quick Facts About the UK

- **Official Name:** The United Kingdom of Great Britain and Northern Ireland
- **Capital City:** London
- **Population:** About 67 million
- **Currency:** British Pound (£)
- **Official Language:** English (plus Welsh, Scots Gaelic, and Irish in some areas)
- **Government:** Constitutional monarchy + parliamentary democracy

MAP OF THE UNITED KINGDOM

Take a look at the map below to see where each of the four countries of the UK are located. You'll also find the capital cities and the seas that surround the islands. This will help you get your bearings before you dive into each region!

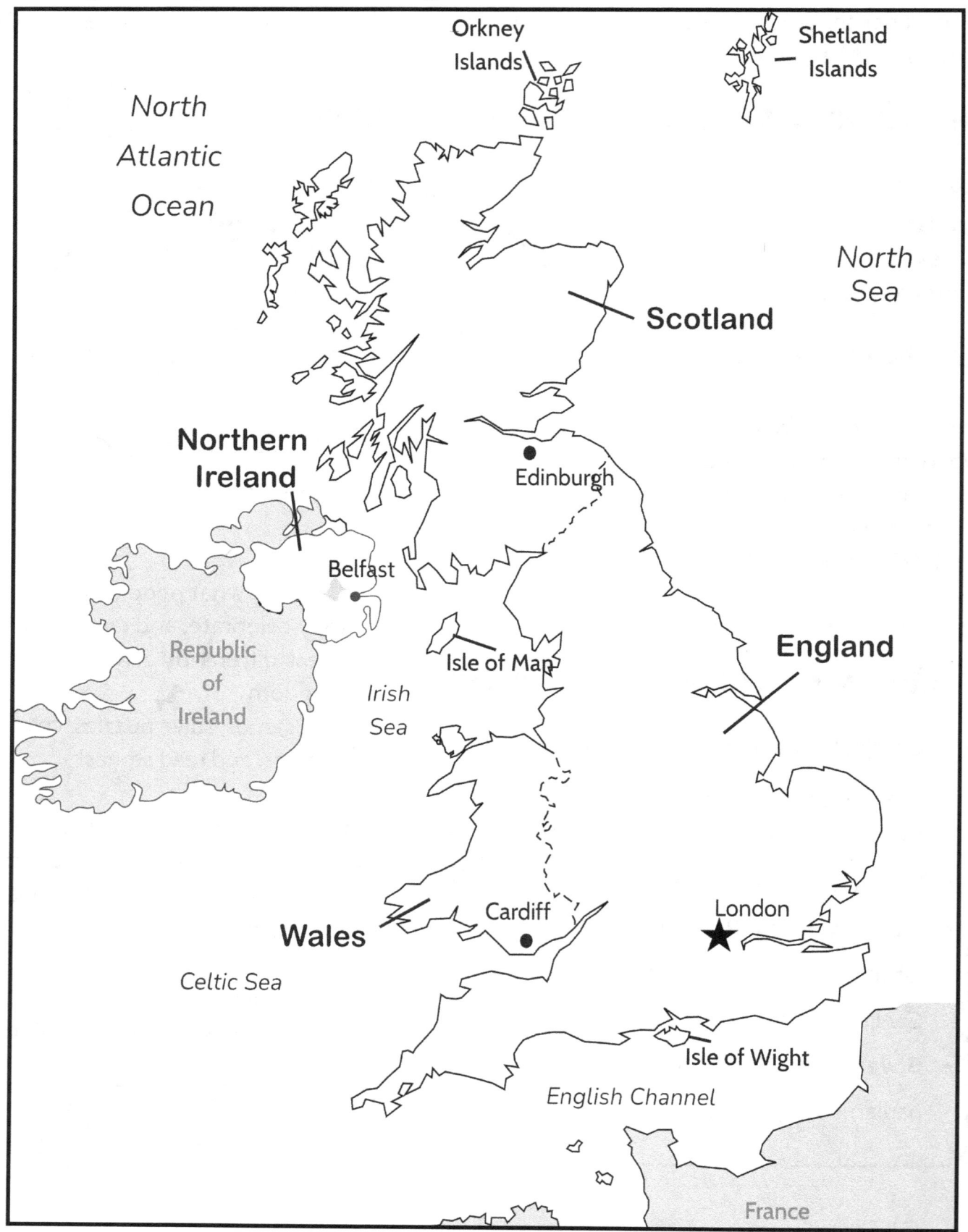

Color the Flag

The Union Jack is the national flag of the United Kingdom. It was first created in 1606 after England and Scotland united under one king. The current design has been used since 1801, when Ireland was added to the United Kingdom. The flag combines parts of the flags of England, Scotland, and Ireland. Wales isn't represented because it was already joined with England when the first version of the flag was created.

Color Guide: Background: Blue; Big central cross: Red; Diagonal X: Red; Diagonal X behind it: White

 **Did You Know?**

- The UK is home to over 1,500 castles!
- The London Underground is the oldest subway system in the world.
- Queen Elizabeth II ruled for over 70 years—the longest reign in UK history.
- People in the UK drink over 100 million cups of tea every day!

Timeline of Major Events

- **c. 3000 BCE** — Stonehenge is built!
- **43 CE** — Romans invade and build cities like Londinium (now London).
- **1066** — William the Conqueror wins the Battle of Hastings.
- **1215** — Magna Carta signed. An early step toward modern democracy.
- **1707** — England and Scotland unite to form Great Britain.
- **1801** — The United Kingdom is officially formed.
- **1922** — Most of Ireland becomes independent; Northern Ireland stays in the UK.
- **Today** — The UK is a modern country with a king, a prime minister, and four nations.

Stonehedge is one of the oldest and most mysterious monuments in the world! Built over 5,000 years ago, no one is quite sure how people moved the massive stones—or why they did it.

Mini Quiz: How Well Do You Know the UK?

1. How many countries make up the United Kingdom?
2. What is the capital of Scotland?
3. True or False: The Republic of Ireland is part of the UK.
4. Which sea lies between Ireland and Great Britain?
5. What colors are used in the Union Jack?

Talk Like a Brit!

Instructions: Draw lines to match each British English word on the left with its American English equivalent on the right. Then complete the bonus activity below!

British English   American English

1. Lift   A. Line
2. Biscuit   B. Soccer
3. Flat   C. Cookie
4. Petrol   D. Flashlight
5. Lorry   E. Elevator
6. Queue   F. Gas
7. Jumper   G. Apartment
8. Football   H. Truck
9. Torch   I. Sweater

Bonus Challenge: Write a short sentence using at least 3 British English words from above.

United Kingdom Word Search

```
O F U N I O N J A C K U P C T
E M K W H M C H A N N E L T D
N B R I T I S H M H D J X C K
O S E X N Z C S G M H B D P A
P A F D W G X R B B L O G L W
A M B U S L U A G N E E U Q M
R V L S X B O L M M M X M O D
L E B M N E G N E H E N O T S
I F Q I A Q C W D H P Y J Z S
A U D D Y G I A O O H N D I S
M E C N W Y N C S C N J D E B
E D U A J I U A R T S B L F E
N N L L O O Y A C E L A U F L
T A T T G R N D L A W E V I F
P L U O H O B S R W R P S D A
J G R C M H I P R G K T M R S
V N E S C D N A L E R I A A T
K E G W X L G G A L F B C C X
```

Belfast	England	Monarchy
British	Flag	Parliament
Cardiff	Ireland	Queen
Castles	Isles	Scotland
Channel	King	Stonehenge
Culture	London	Union Jack
Edinburgh	Magna Carta	Wales

Government

The United Kingdom is a constitutional monarchy and a parliamentary democracy. That means the country has a king or queen, but they don't make the laws — the government does.

The UK's laws are made in a place called Parliament, which meets in the Palace of Westminster in London. Inside Parliament, there are two groups called the House of Commons and the House of Lords. Members of Parliament (MPs) are elected by the people to speak for them and make decisions.

The leader of the government is called the Prime Minister, who is chosen from the elected MPs. The Prime Minister works with a group of officials called the Cabinet to run the country.

Even though the king (currently King Charles III) is the head of state, the government runs most day-to-day affairs. Everyone has to follow the rule of law, and people can vote in elections to choose their leaders.

King Charles III

A Short History of England

England has a rich history stretching back thousands of years. It was first settled by Celtic tribes before being conquered by the Romans, who built roads, cities, and Hadrian's Wall in the north. After the Romans left, waves of invaders arrived—Anglo-Saxons, Vikings, and finally the Normans, whose victory at the Battle of Hastings in 1066 changed the country forever.

In 1215, English nobles forced King John to sign the Magna Carta—a key moment in shaping the idea of individual rights. During the 1500s, Queen Elizabeth I led England through a golden age of exploration, theater, and trade. Later, England became part of the United Kingdom and played a major role in the Industrial Revolution, inventing machines, railways, and global trade networks.

Today, England is known for its castles, inventions, famous writers, and its royal family.

Map of England

Color the Flag

The Flag of England is known as the St. George's Cross. It features a bold red cross on a plain white background. The flag dates back to the Middle Ages and is named after Saint George, England's patron saint. According to legend, Saint George was a brave knight who fought a dragon to save a princess. His red cross became a symbol of courage and was used by English soldiers during the Crusades. Over time, the red cross became the official flag of England.

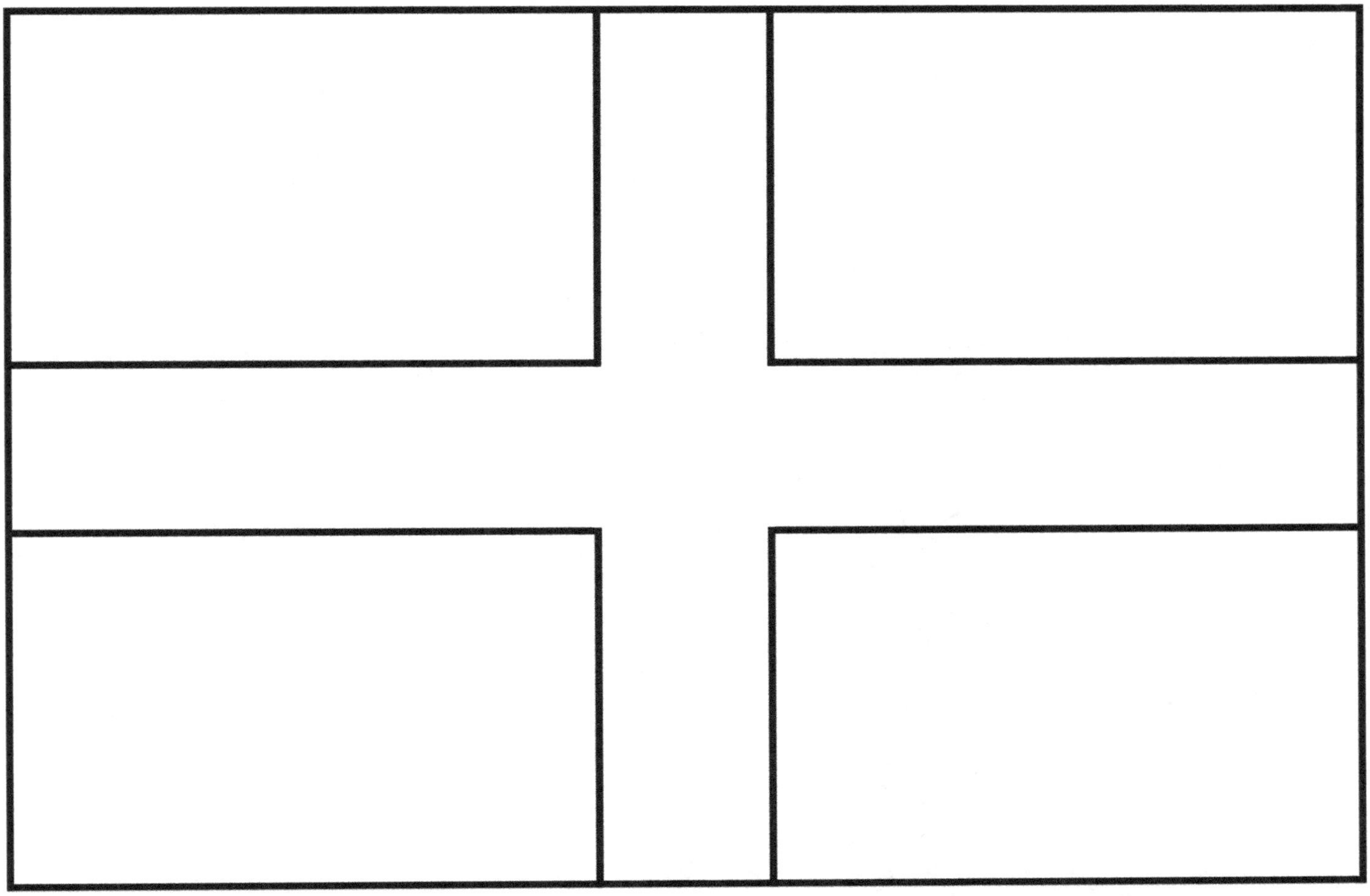

Quick Facts about England

- **Capital:** London
- **Population:** About 58 million
- **Famous Landmarks:** Big Ben, Tower of London
- **Famous River:** Thames
- **Popular Sports:** Football (soccer), cricket, rugby
- **Patron Saint:** Saint George
- **National Day:** April 23 (St. George's Day)
- **Famous Foods:** Fish and chips, roast dinner, Yorkshire pudding

The Magna Carta, or "Great Charter," was a special document signed in 1215 by King John of England. At the time, many people were unhappy with the king's unfair rules and high taxes. A group of powerful nobles forced him to agree to a set of laws that would limit his power. The Magna Carta said that even the king had to follow the law—and that people had rights the king couldn't take away.

Although the Magna Carta was written over 800 years ago, it's still famous today because it helped inspire ideas like freedom, fairness, and justice. Many of the rights in modern democracies—like the right to a fair trial—can be traced back to this important moment in English history.

England Word Search

```
Z X C I U B Y T L A Y O R Y I
A Z K R E T T O P Y R R A H W
W E S T M I N S T E R X X Q O
D N E B G I B Y I Q E E X S M
Q O F O O T B A L L R K T E A
W S U T C D Z E X A I E O N H
W R G B N R M B E K H C W G G
I M K G L I O P S S S A E L N
M E R T T E S W D B K L R A I
B R L A N E D L N W R A B N K
L T E I K T O E S D O P R D C
E T A A Z W H M C W Y O I L U
D L H V S A K A Y K X K D O B
O S Z T P A B X M Y E Y G N U
N X O S V V R E X E L R E D K
Q C A T J O R A T F S R T O U
U O X F O R D D B H T P G N V
```

Big Ben	England	Shakespeare
Buckingham	Football	Tea Time
Cambridge	Harry Potter	Thames
Cotswolds	London	Tower Bridge
Crown	Oxford	Westminster
Double Decker	Palace	Wimbledon

Symbols of England

National Animal — Lion

National Flower — Rose

National Bird — Robin

ENGLISH TIMELINE

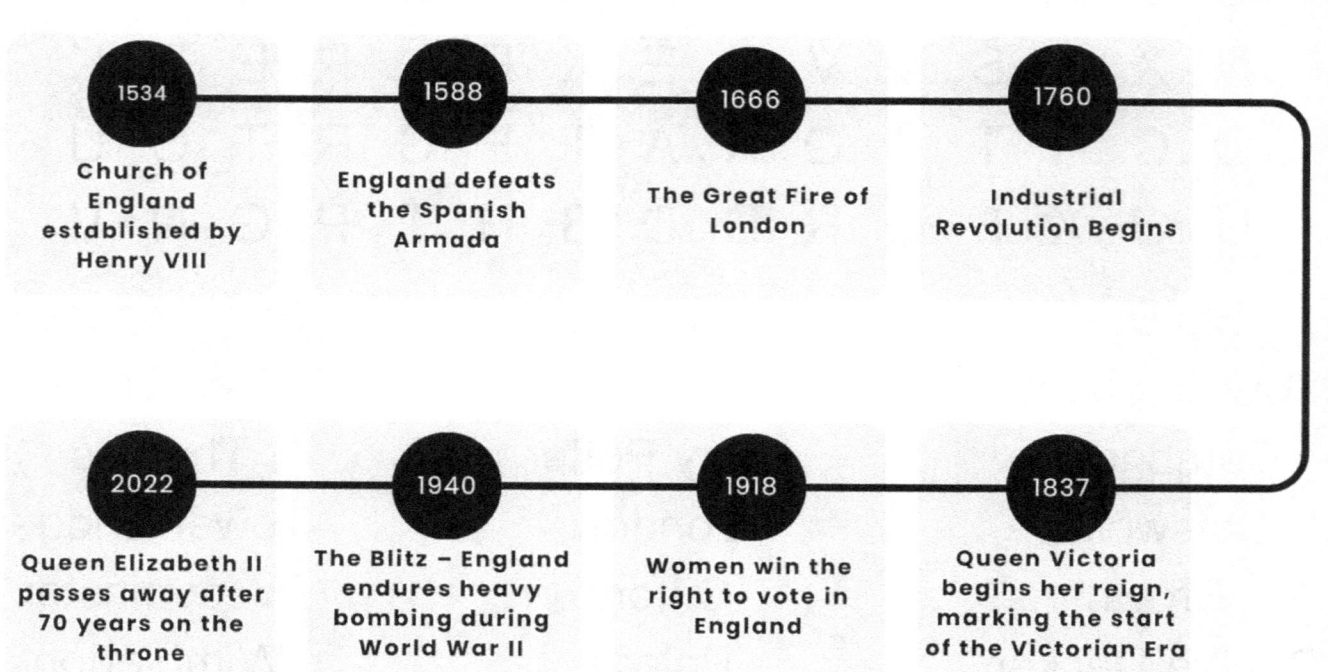

- **1534** — Church of England established by Henry VIII
- **1588** — England defeats the Spanish Armada
- **1666** — The Great Fire of London
- **1760** — Industrial Revolution Begins
- **1837** — Queen Victoria begins her reign, marking the start of the Victorian Era
- **1918** — Women win the right to vote in England
- **1940** — The Blitz – England endures heavy bombing during World War II
- **2022** — Queen Elizabeth II passes away after 70 years on the throne

Landmark Matching Game

Match the landmarks with their descriptions.

 **Windsor Castle**

A famous clock tower in London.

 **White Cliffs of Dover**

A long stone wall built by the Romans.

 **Globe Theatre**

A medieval fortress and former royal palace.

 **London Tower**

A round theater where Shakespeare's plays were performed.

 **Big Ben**

Steep cliffs on England's southern coast.

 **Hadrian's Wall**

A royal residence for more than 900 years.

Famous People from England

England has been home to many world-changing thinkers, artists, scientists, and leaders. Meet some of the most famous!

William Shakespeare

William Shakespeare is often called the greatest writer in the English language. Born in 1564 in Stratford-upon-Avon, he wrote plays that are still performed around the world today. Some of his most famous works include *Romeo and Juliet*, *Hamlet*, and *Macbeth*. His plays are filled with drama, humor, and unforgettable characters.

Shakespeare also wrote 154 sonnets (short poems), and he helped shape modern English with new words and phrases that we still use today. He lived during the reign of Queen Elizabeth I and performed many of his plays at the Globe Theatre in London.

Isaac Newton

Sir Isaac Newton was one of the greatest scientists of all time. Born in 1642 in England, he changed how we understand the universe. He discovered the laws of motion and gravity — the reason why apples fall and planets stay in orbit! Newton also helped invent a type of math called calculus.

He was curious about everything: light, color, astronomy, and how things move. His most famous book, *Principia Mathematica*, explained the laws of physics and became one of the most important science books ever written.

Florence Nightingale

Florence Nightingale is known as the founder of modern nursing. Born in 1820 in England, she became famous during the Crimean War, when she helped care for wounded soldiers. She worked long hours in dangerous conditions and became known as "The Lady with the Lamp" because she visited the sick at night with a lantern.

After the war, Florence helped improve hospitals around the world by teaching better ways to keep them clean and organized. She also started a nursing school and helped make nursing a respected profession. Her work saved thousands of lives and changed health care forever.

Charles Darwin

Charles Darwin was a naturalist who changed the way people think about animals, nature, and even humans. Born in 1809 in England, Darwin spent five years sailing around the world on a ship called the HMS Beagle. During his travels, he studied animals and plants—especially on the Galápagos Islands.

From his research, Darwin developed the theory of evolution by natural selection, which he explained in his famous book *On the Origin of Species*. His ideas were surprising at the time, but they helped scientists understand how living things change and adapt over time.

Winston Churchill

Winston Churchill was the Prime Minister of the United Kingdom during World War II and is remembered for his strong leadership and powerful speeches. Born in 1874, Churchill led Britain through some of its darkest days as it fought against Nazi Germany. His famous words like "We shall never surrender" inspired the nation to stay strong.

Churchill was not only a wartime leader—he was also a writer, painter, and winner of the Nobel Prize in Literature. He served in the military, held many government positions, and returned as Prime Minister again in the 1950s. He is remembered as one of Britain's greatest leaders.

Queen Elizabeth II

Queen Elizabeth II was the longest-reigning monarch in British history, serving as queen from 1952 until her death in 2022. She became queen at just 25 years old and led the United Kingdom through decades of major change, including the end of the British Empire and the rise of the internet age.

Respected for her sense of duty and calm presence, Queen Elizabeth met world leaders, visited over 100 countries, and became a symbol of unity and tradition. She was known for her colorful outfits, royal wave, and love of corgis and horses. Millions around the world admired her quiet strength and lifelong dedication to her country.

Traditions and Customs of England

Guy Fawkes Night (Bonfire Night)

Every year on November 5th, people across England light bonfires and set off fireworks to remember a failed plot from over 400 years ago. In 1605, a man named Guy Fawkes tried to blow up the Houses of Parliament. Luckily, the plot was stopped just in time.

To celebrate, communities gather for fireworks shows, eat toffee apples, and even burn pretend "Guys" on the fire. Some people still recite the old rhyme: "Remember, remember the 5th of November!"

Changing of the Guard

Outside Buckingham Palace, you can watch a famous royal tradition called the Changing of the Guard. It's when the guards in red coats and tall black hats (called bearskins) switch shifts—complete with music and marching!

This event happens on select days and draws huge crowds. The guards look serious, but it's an exciting sight full of British pageantry and precision.

Afternoon Tea

Afternoon tea started in the 1800s with a duchess who got hungry between lunch and dinner—and it caught on fast! Today, it's a special treat where people enjoy tea with tiny sandwiches, sweet scones, and mini cakes.

This tradition is often served on a three-tiered tray and accompanied by fancy china cups. Kids especially love the scones topped with jam and clotted cream—yum!

Maypole Dancing

In spring, especially around May Day (May 1st), children in villages dance around a tall wooden pole decorated with colorful ribbons. This tradition, called Maypole dancing, celebrates the return of warmer weather and new life.

As music plays, each dancer holds a ribbon and weaves around the pole in a pattern. At the end, the ribbons are beautifully braided down the pole. It's a cheerful event filled with laughter, flowers, and community fun.

The Legend of Robin Hood

LONG AGO, in the time of kings and castles, there lived a young man named Robin of Locksley in merry old England. Robin had grown up in Sherwood Forest, where the ancient oak trees stretched their mighty branches toward the sky and deer grazed peacefully in sun-dappled meadows.

But these were troubled times. The good King Richard had gone away to fight in distant lands, leaving his greedy brother Prince John to rule in his place. Prince John cared nothing for the common people. He raised taxes so high that families couldn't afford to buy bread, and he sent his cruel Sheriff of Nottingham to collect every last coin from the poor.

One autumn day, Robin witnessed something that changed his life forever. He saw the Sheriff's men taking the last few silver pieces from a widow who could barely feed her children. Her tears sparkled in the sunlight as she begged them to leave her something, anything, so her little ones wouldn't go hungry.

"This isn't right," Robin declared, stepping forward. He was skilled with a bow and arrow, having learned to hunt in the forest, and he was quick with his sword. "You've taken enough from these good people."

The Sheriff's men laughed at the young man who dared to challenge them. But Robin was determined to help. That day, he made a choice that would make him an outlaw—but also a hero.

Robin gathered around him other brave souls who believed in fairness and justice. There was Little John, who despite his name was the tallest and strongest man in all of Sherwood. There was Friar Tuck, a jolly monk who could swing a staff as well as he could sing a hymn. Will Scarlet brought his quick wit and quicker sword, while Alan-a-Dale enchanted everyone with songs and stories around the campfire.

Together, they became known as Robin Hood's Merry Men, and they made their home deep in Sherwood Forest, where the Sheriff's soldiers feared to venture. They built clever hideouts in hollow trees and learned every secret path through the woods.

Robin and his friends had a simple but powerful mission: they would take from the rich who had too much, and give to the poor who had too little. They weren't thieves seeking gold for themselves—they were fighting to make things fair again.

Their most daring adventures often involved the Sheriff of Nottingham himself. Robin would disguise himself as a merchant or a traveling minstrel, then surprise the Sheriff's tax collectors on the forest roads. With a twang of his bowstring and a flash of his sword, Robin would redistribute the stolen coins back to the families who needed them most.

The Sheriff grew furious. He posted wanted signs throughout the land: "REWARD for Robin Hood, Dead or Alive!" But the common people loved Robin, and no one would betray him. Instead, they would warn him when the Sheriff's men were coming, and help him escape through hidden forest trails.

One of Robin's most famous tricks happened during an archery contest in Nottingham. The Sheriff had organized the tournament, hoping to lure Robin out of hiding with the promise of a golden arrow as the prize. Robin couldn't resist the challenge, even though he knew it was a trap.

Disguising himself with a false beard and peasant clothes, Robin entered the contest. Archer after archer stepped forward, sending their arrows toward the distant target. But when Robin's turn came, his arrow flew straight and true, splitting the previous best shot right down the middle—a feat so incredible that the crowd gasped in amazement.

As the Sheriff prepared to award the prize, he suddenly realized who this mysterious archer must be. "Seize him!" he shouted. "That's Robin Hood!"

But Robin was already moving. With a laugh and a flourish, he pulled off his disguise and bowed to the cheering crowd. "Thank you for a lovely afternoon!" he called out, then disappeared into the forest before the guards could react.

The adventures continued for many years. Robin and his Merry Men rescued prisoners from the Sheriff's dungeons, protected travelers from bandits, and made sure that no family in their part of England went hungry. They became so famous that minstrels sang songs about them in taverns throughout the land.

Eventually, the good King Richard returned from his travels. When he heard about Robin Hood's deeds, the wise king realized that Robin had been fighting for justice all along. Instead of punishing him, King Richard pardoned Robin and his friends, praising them for protecting his people when he couldn't be there to do it himself.

The Sheriff of Nottingham, on the other hand, was stripped of his position and sent away in disgrace.

Robin Hood had proven that sometimes, when the world seems unfair, ordinary people can make extraordinary differences. He showed that courage, friendship, and standing up for what's right are more valuable than all the gold in the kingdom. And though Robin Hood lived long ago, people still tell his story today.

The legend says that on quiet mornings in Sherwood Forest, if you listen carefully, you might still hear the whisper of an arrow flying through the air and the echo of Robin's laughter carried on the wind—a reminder that the spirit of justice and kindness lives on forever.

A Short History of Scotland

Scotland has a long and proud history that began thousands of years ago with Celtic tribes and mysterious standing stones. Later, the Romans built Hadrian's Wall to keep out fierce Scottish warriors, who they called the Picts. Over time, powerful clans ruled the land, and brave leaders like William Wallace and Robert the Bruce fought to keep Scotland free from English control.

In 1314, the Scots won a major victory at the Battle of Bannockburn, and Scotland remained independent for centuries. But in 1707, Scotland joined with England to form the United Kingdom. Even after that, Scottish culture, traditions, and language stayed strong.

Today, Scotland is known for its castles, mountains, bagpipes, and tartan kilts. It has its own parliament and proudly celebrates its unique identity as part of the UK.

Map of Scotland

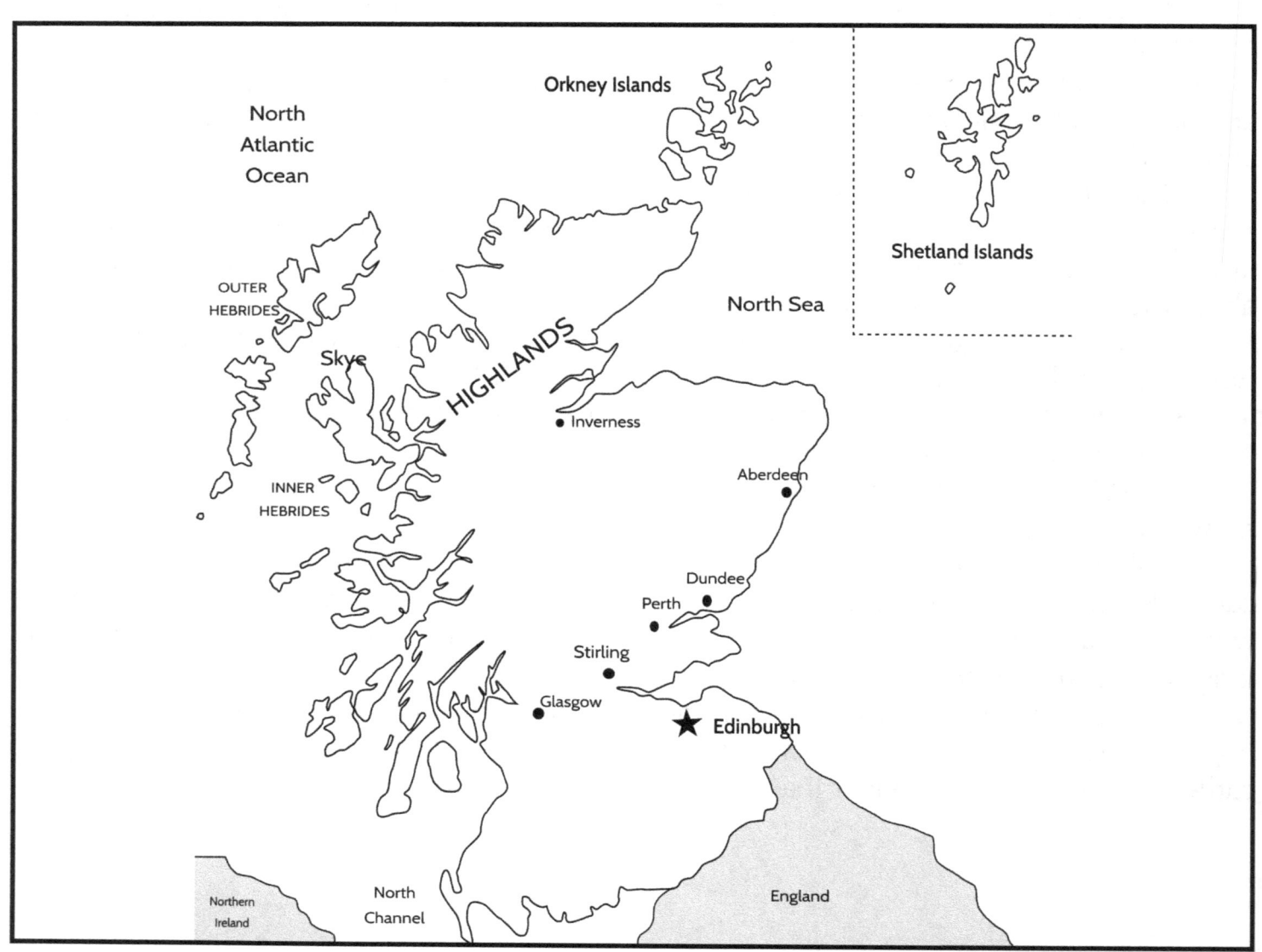

Color the Flag

The flag of Scotland is called the Saltire or St. Andrew's Cross. It features a bold white X-shaped cross on a bright blue background. The cross represents Saint Andrew, the patron saint of Scotland, who was said to have been martyred on a diagonal cross.

It's one of the oldest flags in the world and has been a proud symbol of Scotland for hundreds of years. Use blue for the background and leave the cross white when you color it in!

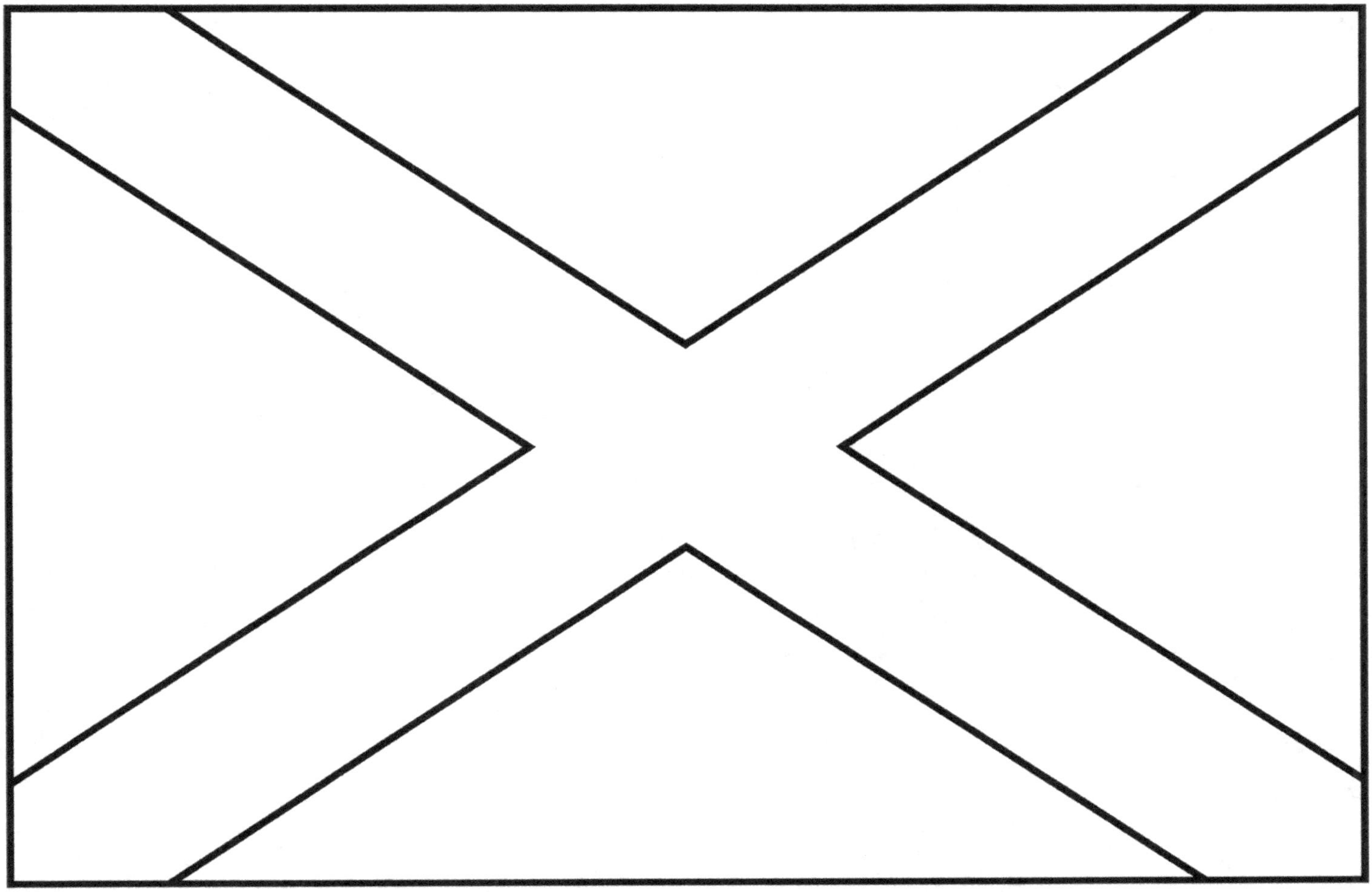

Quick Facts about Scotland

- **Capital:** Edinburgh
- **Cities:** Glasgow, Abderdeen, Dundee, Inverness
- **Population:** About 5.5 million
- **Famous Landmarks:** Edinburgh Castle, Loch Ness, The Kelpies
- **Famous River:** River Clyde
- **Highest Mountain:** Ben Nevis
- **Official Languages:** English, Scottish Gaelic, Scots
- **National Dish:** Haggis

The Battle of Bannockburn

In the year 1314, a great battle took place near the town of Stirling in Scotland. The Scottish army, led by **Robert the Bruce**, faced a much larger English force. The English king wanted to take control of Scotland, but the Scots were determined to stay free. Robert the Bruce chose a smart location and used clever tactics to win. His soldiers fought bravely, even though they were outnumbered. On the second day of battle, the Scottish forces pushed the English army back—and won a huge victory. **The Battle of Bannockburn** became one of the most important moments in Scottish history. It showed that Scotland would not give up its independence without a fight.

Scotland Word Search

```
Z S W N G N D X E S C N T H I
J E S O Z C C V S F A U G O H
V P T D U W E E M T U R U E I
T I E H V T N I R Y U M N G N
J P M D I H L A L B I Z I L V
X G G C C S T A N I Z I C A E
S A B O E L T I N O D H O S R
W B L C A A D L L D S H R G N
E F O V P E A F E S E Z N O E
R I S L E O F S K Y E R T W S
D A N S N A L C A U W A Q U S
N Q V Q U S G S C O T L A N D
A B U S I V E N N E B K V S A
T H E A T H E R F A S I U I R
S I C O Z H T B B D G L V G Z
P A U L W T W E E D X T F G K
E I S S E N V X N Y W S Y A K
F B R C S D N A L H G I H H B
```

Bagpipes	Heather	Outlander
Ben Nevis	Highlands	Scotland
Ceilidh	Inverness	St Andrews
Clans	Isle Of Skye	Tartan
Edinburgh	Kilts	Thistle
Glasgow	Loch Ness	Tweed
Haggis	Nessie	Unicorn

Symbols of Scotland

National Animal

Unicorn

National Flower

Thistle

National Bird

Golden Eagle

SCOTTISH TIMELINE

- **c. 843** — Kingdom of Scotland is formed under Kenneth MacAlpin
- **1314** — Battle of Bannockburn – Robert the Bruce wins Scottish independence
- **1603** — Union of the Crowns – James VI of Scotland becomes King of England
- **1746** — Battle of Culloden – end of the Jacobite Rebellions
- **1822** — King George IV visits Scotland – tartan becomes a national symbol
- **1843** — The Disruption – Scottish church splits into two major groups
- **1999** — Scottish Parliament established for the first time in nearly 300 years
- **2014** — Scotland votes No in independence referendum

Landmark Matching Game

Match the landmarks with their descriptions.

 **Edinburgh Castle**

A red railway bridge and engineering marvel near Edinburgh

 **Loch Ness**

Two giant horse-head sculptures near Falkirk, based on Scottish myths

 **Ben Nevis**

A fortress on a hill in Scotland's capital, full of royal history.

 **The Kelpies**

The royal residence in Scotland, at the end of the Royal Mile

 **Forth Bridge**

A deep lake said to be home to the legendary Nessie.

 **Hollyrood Palace**

The highest mountain in the UK, popular with climbers.

Famous People from Scotland

Scotland has been home to many world-changing thinkers, artists, scientists, and leaders. Meet some of the most famous!

William Wallace

William Wallace was a Scottish knight who became a national hero for standing up to English rule. In the 1290s, when Scotland was under threat, Wallace gathered an army and led a surprise victory at the Battle of Stirling Bridge. His bravery and clever tactics helped inspire other Scots to join the fight for independence.

Though he was later captured and executed, Wallace became a symbol of freedom and Scottish pride. His story was passed down for centuries and made famous in the movie *Braveheart*. Today, you can see a huge monument to him near the city of Stirling.

Mary, Queen of Scots

Mary became queen of Scotland when she was just six days old! Her life was full of drama—she married three times, was forced to give up her throne, and spent years in prison. Mary was also the cousin of Queen Elizabeth I of England, which made things even more complicated.

Eventually, Mary was accused of plotting against Elizabeth and was executed in 1587. Though her life ended sadly, she's remembered as one of history's most fascinating royal figures, and her story still captures imaginations today.

Adam Smith

Adam Smith was a Scottish thinker whose ideas helped shape how we understand the economy. In 1776, he wrote a famous book called *The Wealth of Nations*, which explained how businesses and trade work. His ideas are still used by economists today!

Smith believed that people should be free to trade and compete fairly, and that governments should protect those rights. He is often called the father of modern economics, and his work influenced countries all around the world

Elsie Inglis

Elsie Inglis was a Scottish doctor, surgeon, and leader who made history during World War I. At a time when women were not even allowed to serve in most hospitals, she founded the Scottish Women's Hospitals, which helped thousands of soldiers across Europe.

She also worked hard for women's rights and supported the suffrage movement in Scotland. Elsie showed that courage and determination could change the world—and open doors for others.

Sean Connery

Sean Connery was a world-famous actor from Edinburgh, best known for being the very first James Bond. He starred in seven Bond films, starting with *Dr. No* in 1962, and helped make the character a global legend.

Connery later appeared in many other movies and won an Oscar for *The Untouchables*. Proud of his Scottish roots, he often spoke about independence and his love for Scotland. He's remembered for his talent, charisma, and iconic voice.

Nicola Sturgeon

Nicola Sturgeon made history as the first woman to become First Minister of Scotland. She led the Scottish Government from 2014 to 2023, focusing on education, healthcare, and giving more power to Scotland.

Nicola was also a strong supporter of Scottish independence and helped lead the country through big events like Brexit and the COVID-19 pandemic. Many people admired her for being a calm, confident leader and a powerful voice for Scotland.

Traditions and Customs of Scotland

Highland Games

The Highland Games are like a mix of a sports day and a Scottish festival! Held in towns and villages across Scotland, these events feature traditional competitions like caber tossing (where athletes flip giant wooden logs), tug-of-war, and stone put (a bit like shot put). Competitors often wear kilts, and bagpipes fill the air with music.

But it's not just about strength—there's also dancing, food, and fun for the whole family. The games have been around for hundreds of years and are a great way to celebrate Scottish culture and community spirit.

Bagpipes Music

The bagpipes are one of Scotland's most famous musical instruments. They make a powerful, soaring sound that can be heard at parades, festivals, and even somber events like memorials. The instrument works by blowing air into a bag and pressing it through pipes to create different notes.

Long ago, bagpipes were used to lead soldiers into battle, and today they're still used in ceremonies and celebrations. When a piper in full tartan steps onto the field, the crowd falls quiet—until that first haunting note fills the air!

Ceilidh Dancing

A ceilidh (pronounced "kay-lee") is a lively Scottish social dance party. People of all ages come together to dance in groups, spin partners, and follow energetic steps set to traditional folk music played on fiddles, accordions, and of course—bagpipes!

Ceilidhs are popular at weddings, holidays, and community events. Even if you don't know the moves, someone will guide you. It's not about dancing perfectly—it's about having fun and laughing together.

Haggis

Haggis might sound unusual at first, but it's one of Scotland's most traditional and beloved dishes! Made from a mix of sheep's heart, liver, and lungs, combined with oats, onions, and spices, haggis is cooked inside a sheep's stomach (or a modern casing) and served hot. While that might seem strange, it was a clever way for people long ago to use every part of the animal and avoid waste. When cooked, haggis becomes a crumbly, spicy, and savory dish often enjoyed with mashed potatoes and turnips—called "neeps and tatties" in Scotland!

Haggis is especially popular on Burns Night, celebrated every year on January 25th to honor the Scottish poet Robert Burns. He even wrote a whole poem about haggis, calling it the "great chieftain o' the pudding-race!" During the traditional dinner, the haggis is carried in on a platter while bagpipes play, and someone recites Burns's poem before everyone digs in. Today, there are even vegetarian versions of haggis, so more people can give it a try!

The Spider's Lesson

The cave was cold and damp, filled with the bitter taste of defeat. Robert the Bruce, once proud king of Scotland, sat hunched against the rocky wall. It was the winter of 1306, and he had been hiding for months, fleeing from one defeat to another. The English had crushed his armies six times.

"Perhaps I should give up," Robert whispered to the darkness. "Perhaps Scotland is meant to be ruled by England forever."

His loyal friend James Douglas stirred by their small fire. "My lord, you are the rightful king of Scotland."

"A king without a kingdom," Robert replied bitterly. "What kind of king am I?"

As if in answer, something caught Robert's eye in the flickering firelight. In the corner of the cave, a small spider was trying to spin its web between two rocks. The wind from the cave entrance kept breaking the delicate thread, and the spider's web fell, incomplete.

Robert watched as the tiny creature began again. Once more, the wind caught the thread and broke it. "Even the spiders fail in this cursed place," Robert muttered.

But the spider did not stop. A third time it began, and a third time the web fell. Robert found himself leaning forward, drawn by the creature's persistence.

The spider tried a fourth time, then a fifth, then a sixth. Each time, the web collapsed. Six failures – exactly the same number as Robert's own defeats.

"What will you do now, little one?" Robert asked softly. "Will you give up as I have?"

The spider paused, then began its seventh attempt. This time, it worked more carefully, testing each strand. When the wind gusted, the spider waited patiently for it to calm.

Strand by strand, the web took shape. Robert held his breath as the spider worked. Finally, miraculously, the web was complete. The spider had succeeded on its seventh try, creating a perfect web that shimmered in the morning light.

Robert stared in amazement. "Seven times," he said slowly. "The spider tried seven times before it succeeded."

Robert stood up, his back straight for the first time in months. "James, that spider has just taught me the most important lesson of my life. Failure is not the end – it is practice for success. If a tiny spider can show such determination, how can I, a king of Scotland, do any less?"

James smiled, seeing the fire return to his king's eyes. "Then we fight again?"

"We fight again," Robert declared. "But this time, we fight smarter."

Robert changed his strategy completely. Instead of meeting the English in large battles, he began guerrilla warfare, striking quickly and disappearing into the forests and mountains he knew so well.

The spider's lesson spread throughout Scotland. "Remember the spider," became a rallying cry whispered before battles, reminding fighters that persistence could overcome any obstacle.

Robert's seventh campaign was different. His forces moved like ghosts through the countryside, learning from every encounter and adapting their tactics just as the spider had adapted its web-building.

Years passed, and Robert's persistence paid off. Castle after castle fell to his forces. The culmination came at the Battle of Bannockburn in 1314, where Robert won a decisive victory that secured Scotland's independence.

As Robert stood on the battlefield, watching the English retreat, he thought of the spider in the cave. That tiny creature had taught him that true strength came not from winning every battle, but from refusing to surrender after losing them.

Years later, when Robert was an old king, he would tell his grandchildren about the spider that changed Scottish history.

"Remember, little ones," he would say, "it matters not how many times you fall. What matters is that you get up one more time than you fall down. Sometimes the greatest teachers come in the smallest packages. "

The spider's web was long gone, but its lesson lived on in the heart of Scotland – a reminder that even the smallest creature can inspire the greatest victories, and that true kings are not those who never fall, but those who always rise again.

A Short History of Wales

Wales has a long and proud history, with people living there for thousands of years. The ancient Celts once ruled the land, and many of their traditions and language are still alive today. In the early Middle Ages, Wales was divided into kingdoms like Gwynedd and Powys, each ruled by powerful princes. One of the most famous was **Llywelyn the Great**, who fought to keep Wales independent.

In 1282, Wales was conquered by England's King Edward I, who built mighty castles to control the region. For centuries, the Welsh people resisted English rule. In 1400, **Owain Glyndŵr** led a famous rebellion and is still celebrated as a national hero.

Wales officially united with England in the 16th century. Today, it has its own parliament and strong cultural identity—especially in music, poetry, and the Welsh language, which is still spoken by many people.

Map of Wales

Color the Flag

The flag of Wales features a red dragon standing proudly on a green and white background. The red dragon, or Y Ddraig Goch in Welsh, has been a symbol of Wales for over a thousand years. Some say it represents ancient Celtic warriors; others believe it was used by King Arthur and other legendary leaders. The green and white stripes were added in Tudor times, representing the royal house of Henry VII, who had Welsh ancestry. While the Welsh flag isn't included in the Union Jack (the flag of the United Kingdom), it remains a powerful symbol of Welsh pride and heritage.

Quick Facts about Wales

- **Capital:** Cardiff
- **Cities:** Swansea, Newport, Bangor
- **Population:** About 3.1 million
- **Famous Landmarks:** Caernarfon Castle, Snowdonia National Park, Brecon Beacons
- **Geography:** Snowdon (highest mountain in Wales), Pembrokeshire Coast, River Severn
- **Official Languages:** Welsh and English
- **National Dish:** Cawl (hearty meat and vegetable stew)
- **National Day:** St. David's Day (March 1st)

Caernarfon Castle

Caernarfon Castle is one of the most famous castles in Wales. It was built in the late 1200s by King Edward I of England as part of his plan to control Wales. With its giant stone towers and thick walls, the castle was designed to look strong and powerful—like a royal fortress.

Over the centuries, Caernarfon Castle has seen many important moments in history. In 1969, it was the site of the Prince of Wales's investiture, where Prince Charles received his royal title. Today, the castle is a UNESCO World Heritage Site and a symbol of Welsh pride and strength.

Wales Word Search

```
Y B N E T S B G R N D D M H K
D N I G E C A R D I F F E O E
A J L L N O D W O N S D F W E
K N A A F U B Q I V K I D W L
X W R B N E I S T E D D F O D
X K H H S G Q A S H E E P M L
D M X Q A E U L N M P R M I F
I V S I B R J A Z G P E D P M
V A H W N T P V G T L O L D N
A L Q Y O I W S R E F E X H B
D L C E C B E V D F A S S Y X
T E M K E E L F A R E P J E S
N Y R P R R S D C L A N U Z Y
I S U H B A H B T N K G B G X
A Y G X X R C S O G Z Z O Q L
S N B G W O A O Z Z O X M N M
Q B Y J E C K E N I M L A O C
E N G M E U E U H T U R M Y C
```

Anglesey
Brecon
Cardiff
Castles
Coal Mine
Cymru
Daffodil

Dragon
Eisteddfod
Harps
Language
Leek
Rarebit
Rugby

Saint David
Sheep
Snowdon
Tenby
Valleys
Wales
Welsh Cake

Symbols of Wales

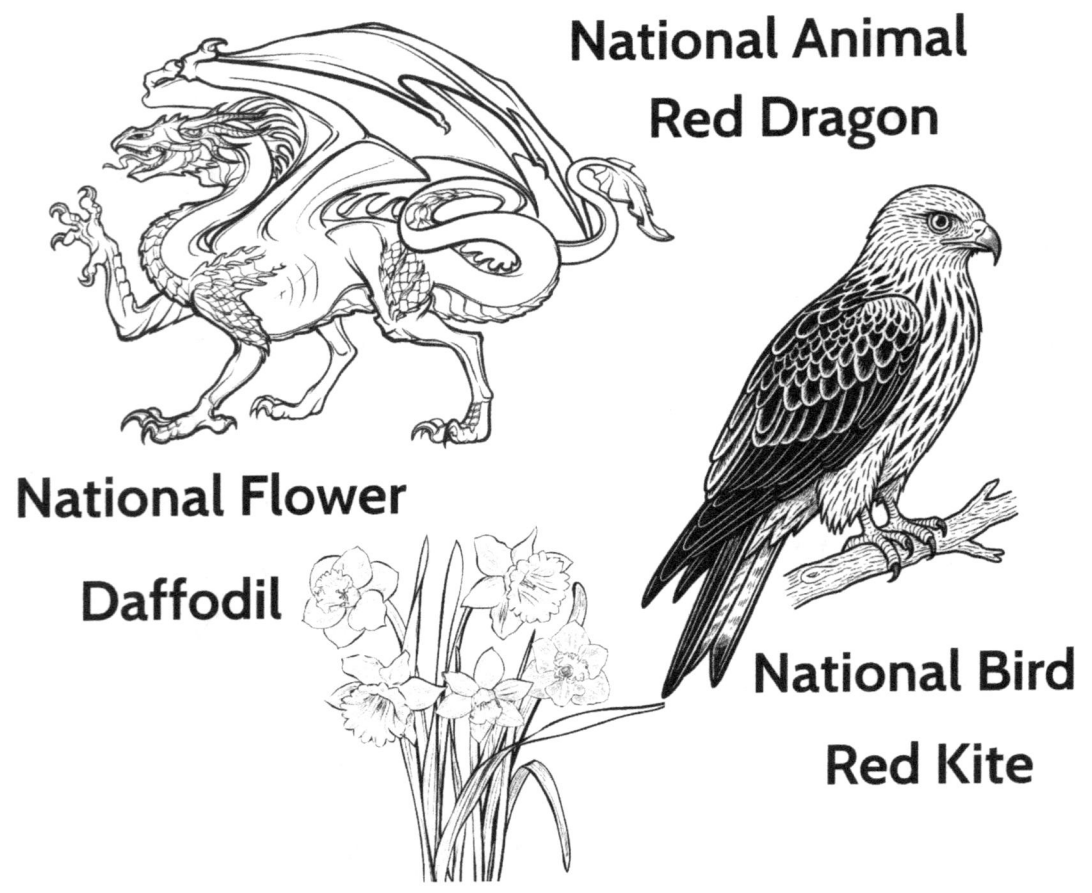

National Animal
Red Dragon

National Flower
Daffodil

National Bird
Red Kite

WALES TIMELINE

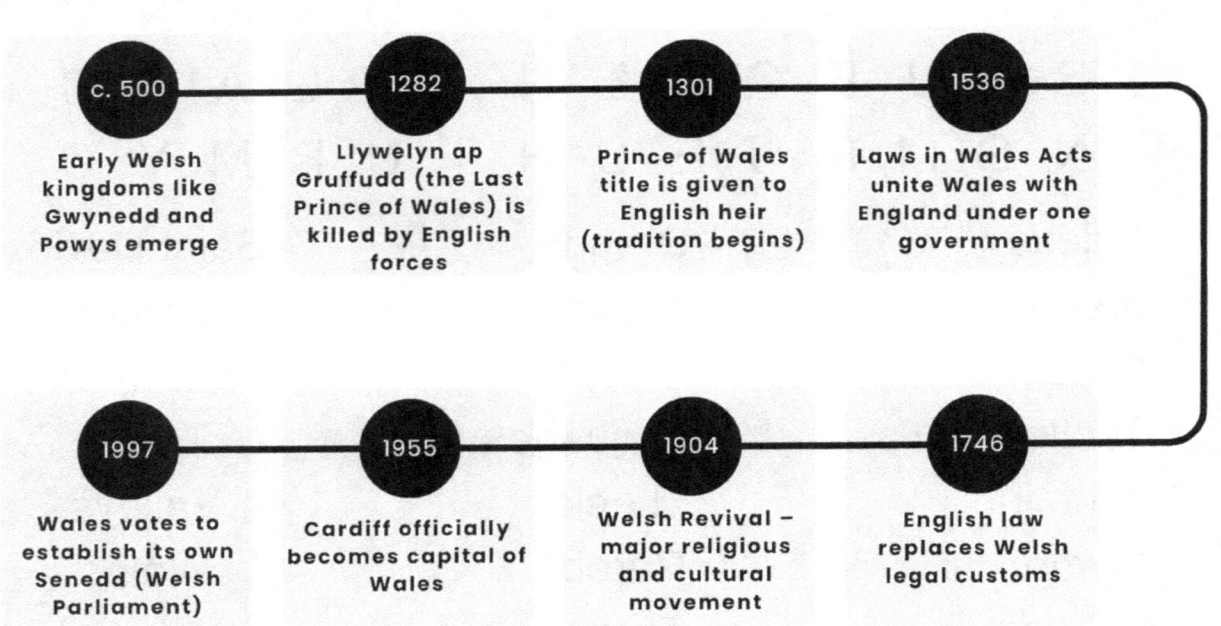

c. 500 — Early Welsh kingdoms like Gwynedd and Powys emerge

1282 — Llywelyn ap Gruffudd (the Last Prince of Wales) is killed by English forces

1301 — Prince of Wales title is given to English heir (tradition begins)

1536 — Laws in Wales Acts unite Wales with England under one government

1746 — English law replaces Welsh legal customs

1904 — Welsh Revival – major religious and cultural movement

1955 — Cardiff officially becomes capital of Wales

1997 — Wales votes to establish its own Senedd (Welsh Parliament)

Landmark Matching Game

Match the landmarks with their descriptions.

 Snowdonia National Park	A religious site honoring Wales' patron saint.
 Cardiff Castle	The modern building where the Welsh Parliament meets.
 St. David's Cathedral	A red-roofed, fairy-tale-style castle in a forest near Cardiff.
 Pembrokeshire Coast	A castle in the capital city with Roman roots and Victorian design.
 The Senedd	Home to Mount Snowdon, the highest peak in Wales.
 Castell Coch	Cliffs, beaches, and coastal wildlife—perfect for nature lovers.

Famous People from Wales

Wales has been home to many world-changing thinkers, artists, scientists, and leaders. Meet some of the most famous!

Owain Glyndwr

Owain Glyndŵr is one of Wales's greatest national heroes. In 1400, he led a major rebellion against English rule and declared himself Prince of Wales. For over a decade, he fought to free Wales, unite the people, and create an independent Welsh parliament and university.

Although his rebellion was eventually defeated, Glyndŵr became a powerful symbol of Welsh pride and resistance. His story is remembered in poems, legends, and even Shakespeare's plays. Today, many people see him as the last true Prince of Wales chosen by the Welsh themselves.

David Lloyd George

David Lloyd George was the first and only Welsh Prime Minister of the United Kingdom, serving during one of the most difficult times in British history—World War I. Born in a small village in North Wales, he rose to the top through hard work, powerful speeches, and bold ideas.

As Prime Minister, he helped lead Britain to victory and later played a key role in the peace talks. He also introduced new laws to help working families and improve health and education. His legacy is still seen today, and he's remembered as one of the most important leaders of the 20th century.

Roald Dahl

Roald Dahl is one of the most beloved children's authors in the world—and he was born in Cardiff, Wales! His books, like *Charlie and the Chocolate Factory*, *Matilda*, and *The BFG*, are full of wild imagination, clever kids, and unforgettable villains.

Dahl served as a pilot in World War II before becoming a writer. He also wrote stories for adults and worked on movie scripts. His playful use of language and love of storytelling continue to inspire generations of young readers.

Catherine Zeta-Jones

Catherine Zeta-Jones is an Oscar-winning actress from Swansea, Wales. She began performing in musicals as a child and went on to star in major films like *Chicago*, *The Mask of Zorro*, and *Ocean's Twelve*.

Known for her talent, grace, and glamorous style, Catherine has become one of the most famous Welsh celebrities in the world. She often speaks proudly of her Welsh roots and continues to support the arts in Wales and beyond.

Ryan Giggs

Ryan Giggs is one of the most famous footballers to ever come from Wales. He spent his entire club career at Manchester United, where he won more trophies than any other British player, including 13 Premier League titles and 2 Champions League cups.

Although Wales never reached the World Cup while he played, Giggs was known for his speed, skill, and loyalty to his team. After retiring, he became a coach and continued to support Welsh football. He remains a role model for many young athletes.

Tanni Grey-Thompson

Tanni Grey-Thompson is a record-breaking Paralympic athlete and one of the UK's most successful wheelchair racers. Born with spina bifida, she began using a wheelchair at a young age—but that didn't stop her from becoming a champion.

Tanni won 11 gold medals across five Paralympic Games and set over 30 world records. After retiring from sports, she became a member of the House of Lords and now works to improve opportunities for disabled people in the UK. Her story is one of strength, determination, and big achievements.

Traditions and Customs of Wales

St. David's Day

St. David's Day is celebrated every March 1st in honor of the patron saint of Wales. On this day, children often dress in traditional Welsh clothing, wear daffodils or leeks on their shirts, and join in school concerts and parades.

St. David was a kind and wise monk who encouraged people to live simply and care for others. Today, his legacy lives on in songs, poetry, and bright yellow flowers that bloom in early spring across Wales.

Rugby Culture

In Wales, rugby is more than just a sport—it's a national passion. On game days, towns and cities come alive with cheers, songs, and red jerseys. The stadium in Cardiff (Principality Stadium) fills with fans waving Welsh flags and singing at the top of their lungs.

Many Welsh children grow up playing rugby at school or in local clubs. Famous players like Gareth Bale and Shane Williams have become national heroes. Whether you're on the field or in the crowd, rugby brings people together in a big, bold way.

Love Spoons

Love spoons are beautifully carved wooden spoons that were traditionally given as gifts to someone special. Each spoon has symbols carved into it—like hearts for love, wheels for support, or knots for togetherness.

This tradition began in Wales hundreds of years ago, and each spoon told its own story. Today, love spoons are still made as decorations or keepsakes, showing how much someone cares in a unique and artistic way.

Eisteddfod – A Celebration of Welsh Arts and Language

The Eisteddfod (pronounced eye-STETH-vod) is one of Wales's oldest and most important traditions. It's a grand festival of poetry, music, and performance that celebrates the Welsh language and culture. The word eisteddfod means "a sitting," and these festivals date all the way back to the 12th century! Today, the National Eisteddfod of Wales is held every summer in different locations and draws thousands of visitors.

Children and adults compete in singing, dancing, storytelling, and poetry—many events are held entirely in Welsh! Winners are crowned with special honors, and the festival includes parades, traditional costumes, food stalls, and fun activities. It's a joyful way to keep Welsh traditions alive and showcase talent from all over the country.

The Red Dragon of Wales

Long ago, when the mountains of Wales were young and the valleys echoed with ancient songs, there lived a boy named Rhys in a small village nestled between rolling green hills. Rhys had grown up hearing the old stories from his grandfather, Taid, who spoke of dragons and magic as if they were as real as the sheep grazing on the mountainsides.

"Tell me again about the dragons, Taid," Rhys would ask every evening as they sat by the fire.

His grandfather's eyes would twinkle in the firelight. "Ah, bachgen," he would say, using the Welsh word for boy, "there were two great dragons that lived deep beneath our land. The Red Dragon of Wales, proud and fierce, protector of our people. And the White Dragon from across the sea, who brought nothing but trouble and sorrow."

Rhys loved these stories, but like many children, he thought they were just tales to pass the long winter nights. That changed during the summer of his twelfth year, when strange things began happening in the valley.

It started with the ground trembling. At first, people thought it might be storms, but the shaking happened even on clear, sunny days. Sheep would bleat nervously and huddle together. The village well began to run dry, and crops withered in the fields despite the regular rain.

"Something is stirring beneath the earth," Taid said one morning, his weathered face creased with worry. "The dragons are waking."

That very night, Rhys was awakened by a sound like thunder rolling through the mountains. But this thunder came from below, not above. He crept to his window and gasped at what he saw.

Rising from a crack in the hillside was an enormous white dragon, its scales gleaming like polished bone in the moonlight. Its eyes burned with cold fire, and when it roared, the sound shattered windows throughout the village. The dragon's breath turned the green grass to ash wherever it touched.

The White Dragon had awakened, and it was angry.

For three days, the creature terrorized the valley. It poisoned streams with its breath, withered crops with its presence, and filled the air with a bone-chilling cold that made summer feel like the depths of winter. The villagers huddled in their homes, too frightened to venture outside.

"Why doesn't someone stop it?" Rhys asked his grandfather on the third night.

Taid placed a gentle hand on his grandson's shoulder. "Only the Red Dragon can stand against the White, but it has been sleeping for so long. Some say it has forgotten its duty to protect Wales."

"Then we need to wake it up," Rhys said with the determination that only a twelve-year-old could muster.

His grandfather looked at him with surprise, then slowly nodded. "The old stories say the Red Dragon sleeps in the deepest cave beneath Mount Snowdon. But the journey is dangerous, especially with the White Dragon prowling the valley."

"I have to try," Rhys said. "I can't just hide while our home is being destroyed."

The next morning, before dawn, Rhys set out for the mountain. He carried his grandfather's walking stick, a pouch of bread and cheese, and most importantly, a small red stone that Taid had given him. "This belonged to my grandfather's grandfather," the old man had said. "It's said to carry the heart of Wales within it."

The journey to Mount Snowdon was treacherous. The White Dragon's presence had turned the familiar paths into a wasteland of withered plants and frozen streams. Twice, Rhys had to hide behind rocks as the great white beast flew overhead, searching for anyone brave or foolish enough to be outside.

Finally, as the sun was setting, Rhys found the cave his grandfather had described. It was a massive opening in the mountainside, so deep that his voice echoed endlessly when he called into it. The air inside felt warm and smelled faintly of smoke and ancient magic.

"Red Dragon!" Rhys called as he ventured deeper into the cave. "Red Dragon of Wales, your people need you!"

For a long moment, there was silence. Then, from the depths of the mountain, came a sound like a great creature stirring from a deep sleep. A rumbling voice echoed through the cavern.

"Who dares wake me from my slumber?"

Rhys's knees shook, but he stood his ground. "I am Rhys, son of Gareth, grandson of Owen. The White Dragon has returned and is destroying our land. Please, we need your help!"

A pair of enormous eyes opened in the darkness, glowing like molten gold. Slowly, the Red Dragon emerged from the shadows, and Rhys gasped at its magnificent size. Its scales were the color of rubies and burnished copper, and flames danced gently around its nostrils. Unlike the White Dragon's cold malice, the Red Dragon radiated warmth and strength.

"I have slept so long," the dragon said, its voice like the rumble of distant thunder. "I had hoped the White Dragon would never return to trouble our land."

"But it has," Rhys said, pulling out the red stone. "And the people of Wales need their protector."

The Red Dragon's eyes focused on the stone, and its expression softened. "You carry the heart of our land, young one. That tells me the old ways are not forgotten." The dragon lowered its great head until it was level with Rhys. "Very well. I will face my ancient enemy once more."

The battle that followed shook the entire valley. The two dragons met in the sky above Mount Snowdon, their roars echoing off the mountains like thunder. The White Dragon breathed ice and despair, turning the air itself into crystalline daggers. But the Red Dragon answered with flames that burned not with destruction, but with the warm light of hope and home.

They fought through the night, neither giving ground. The White Dragon was powerful and cunning, but the Red Dragon fought with the strength of every Welsh heart, every story told by firesides, every song sung in the valleys below.

As dawn broke over the mountains, the Red Dragon managed to wrap its powerful coils around its enemy. "You do not belong in this land," it declared. "Return to the cold seas from whence you came, and trouble Wales no more!"

With a final, furious shriek, the White Dragon was defeated. It dissolved into mist and shadow, banished back to the distant shores across the sea. The Red Dragon landed on the mountainside, breathing heavily but victorious.

"It is done," the great creature said to Rhys, who had watched the battle from the cave entrance. "The White Dragon will not return in your lifetime, or your children's lifetime. But remember this, young guardian of Wales – the Red Dragon's strength comes not from its size or fire, but from the courage and unity of the Welsh people. As long as you remember your stories, your language, and your love for this land, the Red Dragon will always be here to protect you."

With those words, the Red Dragon spread its mighty wings and soared into the morning sky, disappearing into the clouds above Mount Snowdon.

Rhys returned to his village to find the grass green again, the streams running clear, and the sun shining warmly on the valley. His grandfather met him at the village edge with tears of pride in his eyes.

"You did it, bachgen," Taid said, embracing his grandson. "You woke the Red Dragon and saved us all."

From that day forward, Rhys became the village storyteller, just like his grandfather before him. He would tell children about the Red Dragon of Wales, about courage in the face of danger, and about how the old stories carry truth and power within them.

And sometimes, on clear mornings when the mist rose from the valleys, people would swear they could see the silhouette of a great red dragon soaring around the peaks of Mount Snowdon, keeping watch over Wales and all who called it home.

The red stone that Rhys carried that day was passed down through his family for generations, and it's said that as long as it remains in Wales, the Red Dragon will never forget its duty to protect the land and its people. For the heart of Wales beats strong in those who remember their heritage, and in their courage, the Red Dragon finds its greatest strength.

A Short History of Northern Ireland

Northern Ireland shares the island of Ireland with the Republic of Ireland, but it has its own unique history and identity. Thousands of years ago, Celtic tribes lived in the region, and their culture remains strong to this day. In the 1100s, English and Norman invaders began to take control of parts of Ireland.

In the 1600s, English and Scottish settlers arrived during the Plantation of Ulster, changing the region's population and politics. Over time, tensions grew between different religious and political groups.

In 1921, Ireland was divided into two parts. The south became the independent Republic of Ireland, while the six counties in the north became Northern Ireland, remaining part of the United Kingdom. For many years, Northern Ireland faced conflict known as The Troubles, but today it enjoys peace and shares power through its own parliament.

Map of Northern Ireland

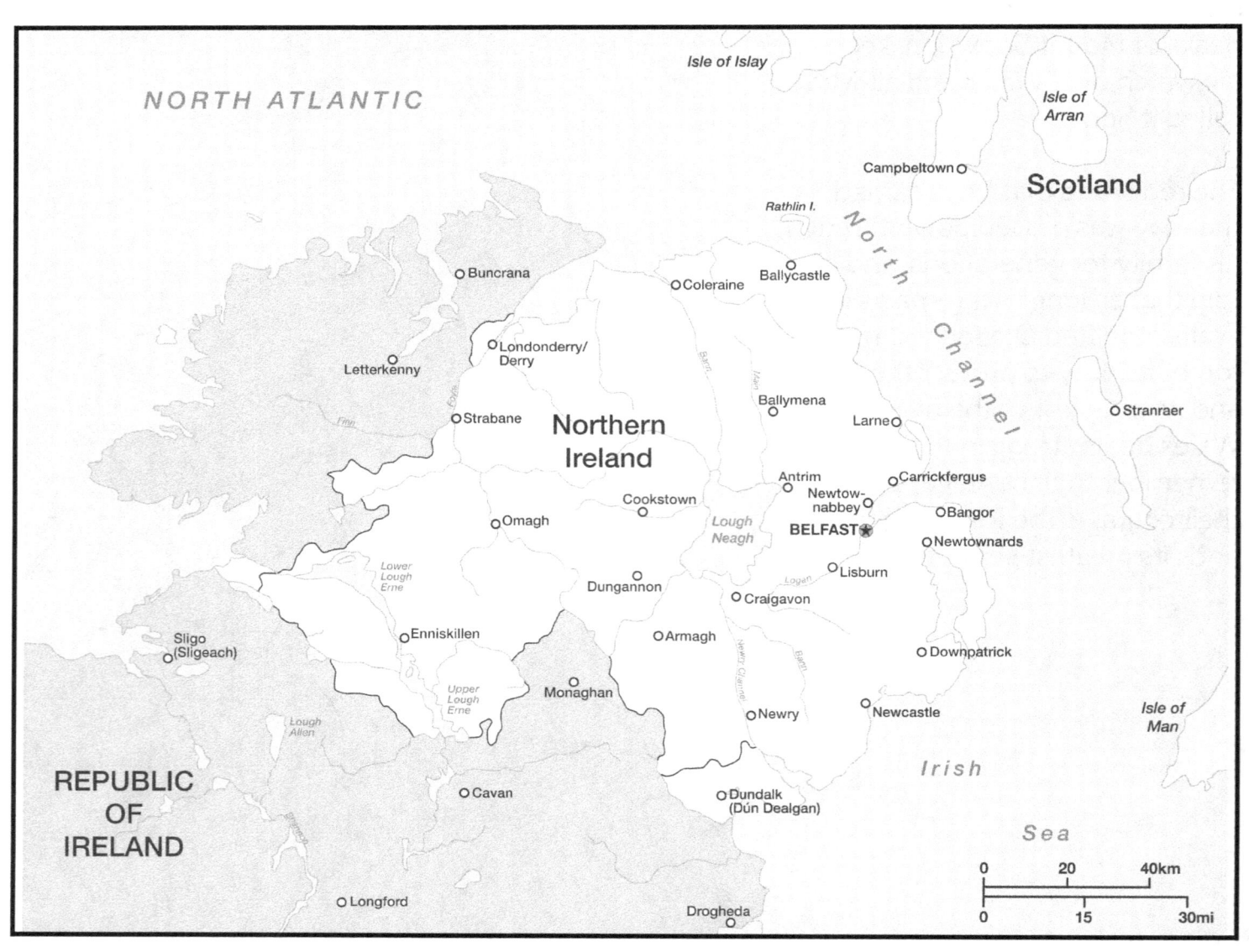

Color the Flag

Northern Ireland does not have an official flag of its own like Scotland or Wales. Instead, the Union Jack (the flag of the United Kingdom) is used for most official purposes. However, in the past, a flag called the Ulster Banner was used by the Northern Ireland government. It features a red cross on a white background, with a red hand in the center and a crown above it. While it's not official today, you might still see the Ulster Banner at sports events.

Color Tip: Red cross and hand, gold crown, white background.

Quick Facts about Northern Ireland

- **Capital:** Belfast
- **Cities:** Derry / Londonderry, Armagh
- **Population:** About 1.9 million
- **Famous Landmark:** Giant's Causeway
- **Geography:** Mourne Mountains, Lough Neagh (largest lake in UK)
- **Languages:** English (Irish and Ulster Scots are also spoken)
- **National Dish:** Ulster Fry
- **National Day:** St. Patrick's Day (March 17)

Giant's Causeway

Over 50 million years ago, a volcano erupted along the Northern Irish coast. When the lava cooled, it cracked into more than 40,000 tall, hexagonal stone columns. Today, this incredible place is called the Giant's Causeway, and it's one of the most famous natural wonders in the world.

But local legend tells a different story. According to Irish myth, a giant named Finn McCool built the stone path to cross the sea and challenge a Scottish giant. When Finn realized how big his rival was, he dressed up as a baby to trick the enemy into thinking that Finn must be enormous if even the baby was that size! The plan worked—and the Scottish giant fled in fear, smashing the causeway behind him. Whether you believe in science or giants (or both), the Giant's Causeway is a magical place to explore.

Northern Ireland Word Search

```
A G K L E I W G A G L P A W Q
D E R R Y V N X N N D D L J A
L R A A O I B I S A L O V E E
Q Q X N C R L S E C O H Q P S
L C P N T R A R M I I G C R H
K L A O U R B N A T J Q I F S
E D L H T A I X G L I F S I I
P M Y Q D A Q M C E J C U D R
E F G O I L T V I C O I M D I
A T S B Y Y S O L E L R Q L E
C C I N A T I T E X G E D E U
E A S K W N T Q A S L L X E H
W B E L F A S T G F X A G P R
A R E T S L U P D Y N N O E B
L I T S Y M I S W A W D L R Q
L K Q R K C O R M A H S F Q E
A I O M G F O L K L O R E P M
L O N D O N D E R R Y I I B S
```

Antrim
Belfast
Celtic
Dancing
Derry
Fiddle
Folklore
Gaelic Games
Golf
Hurling
Ireland
Irish Sea
Londonderry
Music
Orange Order
Peace Wall
Potatoes
Shamrock
Soda Bread
Titanic
Ulster

Symbols of Northern Ireland

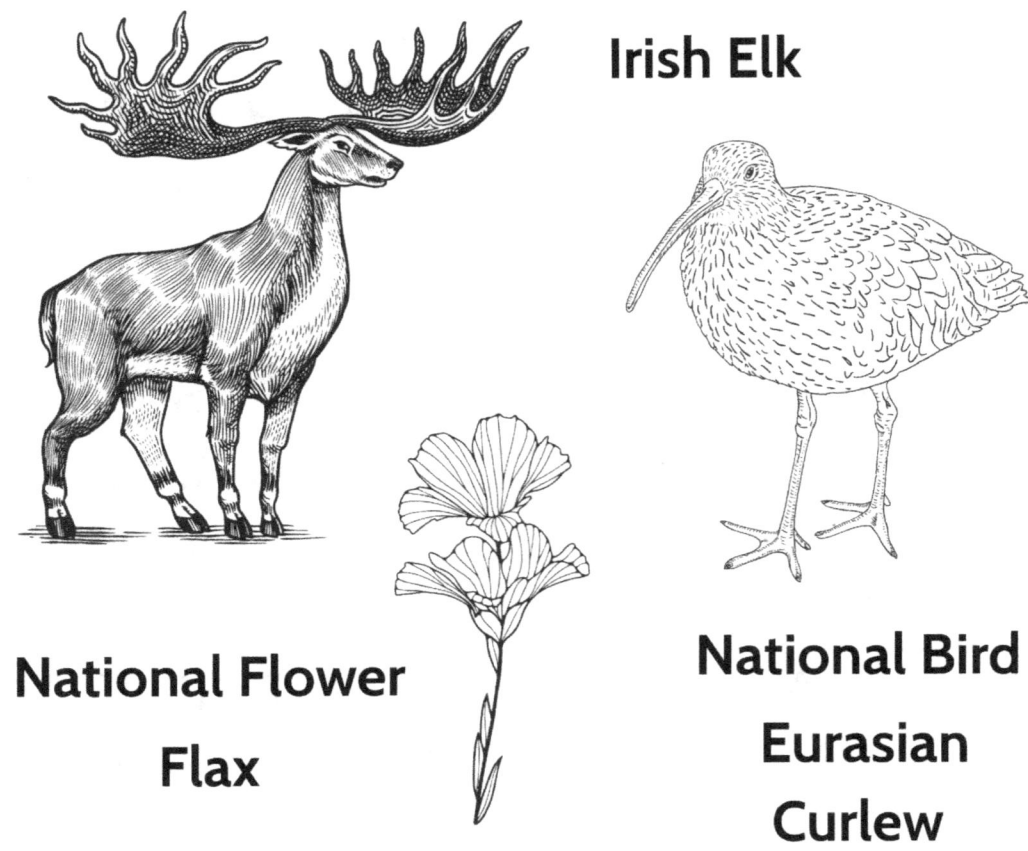

National Animal
Irish Elk

National Flower
Flax

National Bird
Eurasian Curlew

NORTHERN IRELAND TIMELINE

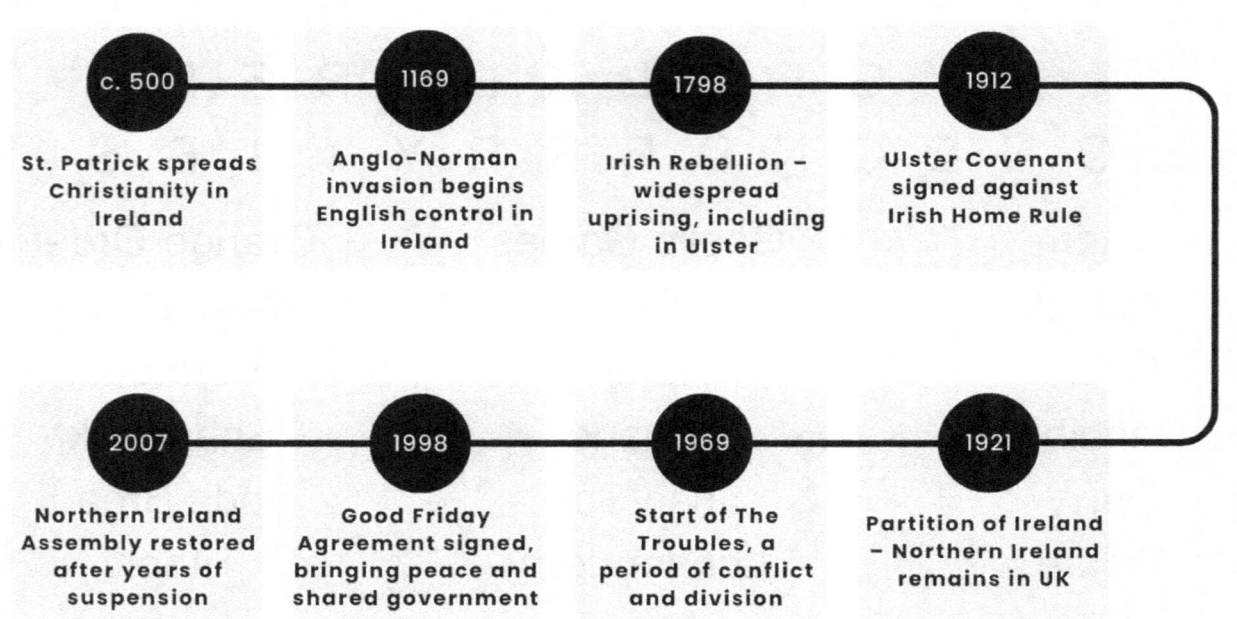

- **c. 500** — St. Patrick spreads Christianity in Ireland
- **1169** — Anglo-Norman invasion begins English control in Ireland
- **1798** — Irish Rebellion – widespread uprising, including in Ulster
- **1912** — Ulster Covenant signed against Irish Home Rule
- **1921** — Partition of Ireland – Northern Ireland remains in UK
- **1969** — Start of The Troubles, a period of conflict and division
- **1998** — Good Friday Agreement signed, bringing peace and shared government
- **2007** — Northern Ireland Assembly restored after years of suspension

Landmark Matching Game

Match the landmarks with their descriptions.

 **Titanic Belfast**

A grand building in the heart of Northern Ireland's capital.

 **Dunluce Castle**

A daring bridge between cliffs over the ocean.

 **Belfast City Hall**

A museum shaped like ship bows, honoring the Titanic.

 **Lough Neagh**

Long murals filled with messages of peace and history.

 **The Peace Walls**

The largest lake in the UK, surrounded by wildlife.

 **Carrick-a-Rede Rope Bridge**

A dramatic ruined castle perched on seaside cliffs.

Famous People from Northern Ireland

Northern Ireland has been home to many world-changing thinkers, artists, scientists, and leaders. Meet some of the most famous!

St. Patrick

St. Patrick is the patron saint of Ireland and one of its most legendary figures. Born in Britain around the year 385, he was kidnapped by pirates as a teenager and taken to Ireland as a slave. After several years, he escaped—but later returned to Ireland as a Christian missionary.

He is credited with bringing Christianity to Ireland and using the shamrock to explain the idea of the Holy Trinity. Though much of his life is wrapped in legend—including tales of him driving snakes out of Ireland—St. Patrick's legacy is celebrated every year on March 17th, known around the world as St. Patrick's Day.

C. S. Lewis

C.S. Lewis was a brilliant author and scholar, best known for writing *The Chronicles of Narnia*. He was born in Belfast in 1898 and loved reading and creating imaginary worlds from a young age. His most famous book, *The Lion, the Witch and the Wardrobe*, has enchanted readers of all ages for decades.

In addition to his fantasy stories, Lewis wrote many books about religion, philosophy, and friendship. He was a professor at Oxford and Cambridge and close friends with other famous writers like J.R.R. Tolkien. Lewis's writing continues to inspire wonder and imagination around the world.

Mary McAleese

Mary McAleese made history as the eighth President of Ireland—and the first person from Northern Ireland to hold the office. Born in Belfast in 1951, she grew up during the early days of the Troubles and became a lawyer and broadcaster before entering politics.

She served as president from 1997 to 2011, focusing on building peace between communities in Northern Ireland and across the island. Her presidency was known as a time of inclusion, education, and progress. She continues to be a powerful voice for peace and human rights.

George Best

George Best was one of the most talented footballers the world has ever seen. Born in Belfast in 1946, he joined Manchester United at just 15 and quickly became a star. He dazzled fans with his speed, skill, and creativity on the field, helping his team win the European Cup in 1968.

Best became a global icon during the 1960s and 70s, admired for both his football and his style. Though his career was marked by ups and downs, his legacy as a football legend lives on. In Belfast, the airport is even named in his honor.

Seamus Heaney

Seamus Heaney was a Nobel Prize-winning poet known for his powerful, moving words. Born in a rural area of Northern Ireland in 1939, he grew up in a farming family and often wrote about nature, home, and history.

Heaney's poems are studied around the world for their beauty and depth. In 1995, he won the Nobel Prize in Literature, and many consider him one of the greatest poets of the 20th century. He believed poetry could help people understand each other—and themselves.

Rory McIlroy

Rory McIlroy is one of the most successful professional golfers of modern times—and he's from Holywood, Northern Ireland. He began playing golf at a very young age and quickly rose through the ranks with his powerful swing and calm focus.

By the time he was in his early 20s, Rory had already won multiple major championships, including the U.S. Open and PGA Championship. He has spent many weeks ranked as the number one golfer in the world and proudly represents Northern Ireland in competitions around the globe.

Traditions and Customs of Northern Ireland

St. Patrick's Day Celebration

St. Patrick's Day is celebrated every March 17th, and it's a big deal in Northern Ireland! People wear green, paint shamrocks on their faces, and enjoy lively parades filled with music, costumes, and Irish dancing.

The holiday honors St. Patrick, who brought Christianity to Ireland. But it's also a joyful celebration of Irish culture, with traditional food, crafts, and storytelling. Whether you're marching in a parade or eating green cupcakes, it's a day to feel proud and festive.

Irish Dancing

Irish dancing is fast, fun, and full of rhythm! Dancers keep their upper bodies still while their feet move quickly in patterns. It's usually performed in colorful dresses and hard shoes that tap on the floor like drums.

Irish dancing is seen at festivals, St. Patrick's Day celebrations, and competitions called feise-anna (pronounced "fesh-uh-nuh"). The energy and precision of the dancers are so exciting, you might just want to jump up and try it yourself!

Twelfth of July Parades

Every summer, the Twelfth of July marks an important historical event: the Battle of the Boyne in 1690. People in some communities in Northern Ireland celebrate with parades, marching bands, and colorful banners.

While it's a day of pride for some, it also reflects the complex history of Northern Ireland. Today, many events focus on music, culture, and celebrating traditions peacefully with family and neighbors.

Ulster Fry

The Ulster Fry is a famous breakfast in Northern Ireland—and it's no small meal! It usually includes bacon, sausage, fried eggs, soda bread, potato bread, and sometimes tomatoes or mushrooms. Everything is cooked in a big frying pan.

It's a hearty meal traditionally eaten on weekends or special occasions. Whether you're climbing a mountain or going to a festival, an Ulster Fry gives you the energy to start your day strong!

The Leprechaun's Last Laugh

Ten-year-old Siobhan O'Brien had always been told she was born with "the sight" — the ability to see things that others couldn't. Her grandmother, Nana Molly, claimed it ran in their family, passed down through generations of Irish women like a precious heirloom.

"It's a gift, mo stór," Nana would say, using the Irish term of endearment that meant "my treasure." "But it's also a responsibility. The fair folk don't appreciate being spied upon by just anyone."

Siobhan wasn't entirely sure she believed in her grandmother's stories about fairies and leprechauns, but she had to admit that she did see strange things sometimes — flickers of movement in her peripheral vision, tiny lights dancing in the garden at twilight, and shadows that seemed to move independently of their owners.

That all changed on a misty morning in County Antrim, when Siobhan was walking through the countryside to visit her cousin Paddy on his family's farm. She had taken the old path that wound through the hills, bordered by ancient stone walls covered in emerald moss and ivy.

As she rounded a bend near a particularly large oak tree, she heard the most peculiar sound: *tap-tap-tap, tap-tap-tap*. It was rhythmic and precise, like someone hammering, but much smaller and quicker than any human craftsman could manage.

Following the sound, Siobhan crept closer to the oak tree. There, sitting cross-legged on a large mushroom at the base of the trunk, was the tiniest man she had ever seen. He was no taller than her hand, dressed in a emerald green coat with brass buttons, brown leather breeches, and a pointed hat with a small feather. His beard was russet red, and his eyes twinkled with mischief.

In his miniature hands, he held an even smaller hammer and was working on what appeared to be a perfectly crafted leather shoe, no bigger than a thimble.

A leprechaun. A real, actual leprechaun.

Siobhan held her breath, remembering Nana Molly's stories. Leprechauns were the cobblers of the fairy world, solitary creatures who made shoes for the other fair folk. They were also notoriously tricky and were said to possess great treasures — pots of gold hidden at the ends of rainbows.

The leprechaun continued his work, completely absorbed in his craft. *Tap-tap-tap, tap-tap-tap*. The tiny shoe was taking beautiful shape under his skilled hands.

Siobhan knew from the stories that if you could catch a leprechaun, he would be obligated to grant you three wishes or tell you where his gold was hidden. But you had to be very careful — leprechauns were clever and would trick you if given the slightest chance.

Taking a deep breath, Siobhan stepped forward and quickly cupped her hands around the tiny man.

"Ah, bless and botheration!" the leprechaun exclaimed in a voice like the tinkling of tiny bells. "Let me go, you great galumphing girl! I've got work to finish!"

"I caught you fair and square," Siobhan said, though her hands were trembling slightly. "That means you have to grant me three wishes or tell me where your gold is hidden."

The leprechaun's eyes narrowed shrewdly. "Caught me, have you? Well, well. It's been many a year since a mortal child has managed that." He stroked his tiny beard thoughtfully. "Very well, I'll honor the old compact. But which will it be — three wishes, or the location of me gold?"

Siobhan considered carefully. Three wishes sounded wonderful, but she had read enough fairy tales to know that wishes often came with unexpected consequences. Gold, on the other hand, seemed more straightforward.

"The gold," she decided. "Tell me where it's hidden."

The leprechaun cackled with delight. "Ah, a practical lass! I like that. Very well, I'll tell you true — me pot of gold is buried beneath the largest stone in the fairy ring on the hill behind your grandmother's cottage."

Siobhan knew the place — a circle of mushrooms that grew on the hill where she and Nana Molly often picked wildflowers. "How do I know you're telling the truth?"

"A leprechaun's word is his bond," the little man said solemnly. "But there's one small catch." His eyes twinkled mischievously.

"What catch?" Siobhan asked suspiciously.

"Well, you see, the gold is definitely there, but it only appears to someone who truly understands its value. Most folks think gold is just shiny metal, but leprechaun gold is different. It represents something far more precious."

Before Siobhan could ask what he meant, the leprechaun twisted in her hands like a wisp of smoke and vanished, leaving only the scent of wild clover and the sound of distant laughter.

Siobhan raced home, her heart pounding with excitement. She found Nana Molly in the garden, tending to her roses.

"Nana! I caught a leprechaun! He told me where his gold is buried!"

Her grandmother looked up with surprise and delight. "Did you now? And where might that be, mo stór?"

"In the fairy ring on the hill! Under the biggest stone!"

Nana Molly wiped her hands on her apron and smiled. "Well then, we'd best go have a look, hadn't we?"

Together, they climbed the hill behind the cottage. The fairy ring was just as Siobhan remembered — a perfect circle of mushrooms with several large stones scattered within it. The biggest stone sat right in the center.

"Help me move this, Nana," Siobhan said, pushing against the heavy stone.

With considerable effort, they managed to roll it aside. Underneath, instead of a pot of gold, they found a small wooden box, weathered with age.

"That's not gold," Siobhan said, disappointed.

"Open it," Nana Molly suggested gently.

Inside the box, Siobhan found a collection of old photographs, letters, and small mementos. As she examined them more closely, she realized they were all connected to her family — pictures of relatives she'd never seen, letters written in her great-grandmother's hand, and a small locket that contained a tiny painting of a woman who looked remarkably like Siobhan herself.

"These are family treasures," Nana Molly said softly, tears glistening in her eyes. "I thought they were lost forever when your great-grandmother's house was sold. How did they end up here?"

As if in answer, a tiny voice whispered on the wind: "Leprechaun gold, young one. More precious than any metal, for it connects you to who you are and where you come from."

Siobhan understood then what the leprechaun had meant. The gold wasn't coins or jewelry — it was something far more valuable. It was her heritage, her family's history, the stories and memories that made her who she was.

"The leprechaun knew," she said wonderingly. "He knew this was here, and he knew it was more important than regular gold."

Nana Molly nodded, holding up a photograph of a young woman in old-fashioned dress. "This is your great-great-grandmother, Siobhan. You're named after her. She had 'the sight' too, and she always said the fair folk were guardians of more than just treasure — they were guardians of memory itself."

As they walked back down the hill, carrying their precious find, Siobhan heard the distant sound of tiny laughter carried on the breeze. She looked back toward the oak tree and thought she caught a glimpse of green coat and pointed hat, but when she blinked, there was nothing there.

"Will I see him again, do you think?" she asked her grandmother.

Nana Molly smiled and tucked a strand of hair behind Siobhan's ear. "The fair folk appear when they're needed, mo stór. You found what you were meant to find today. But keep your eyes open — with 'the sight' and a heart full of wonder, you never know what magic you might discover next."

From that day forward, Siobhan paid closer attention to the whispers in the wind and the shadows that danced at the edges of her vision. And sometimes, when she walked past that old oak tree, she would leave a tiny thimble of milk and a piece of bread by the mushroom where she'd first seen the leprechaun. It was always gone by morning, and occasionally, she'd find a perfectly crafted miniature shoe in its place — a reminder that magic was real, and that some friendships transcended the boundaries between the human world and the realm of the fair folk.

UK Quiz

Test your knowledge about the United Kingdom. Circle the correct answer.

1 What is the capital of Scotland?

a) London
b) Belfast
c) Edinburgh

2 Which country is famous for the red dragon on its flag?

a) Wales
b) Ireland
c) England

3 Where can you visit the Giant's Causeway?

a) Wales
b) Northern Ireland
c) Scotland

4 What food is haggis most associated with?

a) Wales
b) England
c) Scotland

5 Which UK country celebrates Guy Fawkes Night with fireworks?

a) England
b) Scotland
c) Northern Ireland

6 What is the national flower of Wales?

a) Thistle
b) Daffodil
c) Rose

7 Which famous clock tower stands in London?

a) Big Ben
b) Ben Nevis
c) The Shard

8 Which UK country's patron saint is Saint Patrick?

a) Scotland
b) Northern Ireland
c) Wales

9 What kind of animal is Nessie, the Loch Ness Monster?

a) A giant cat
b) A mythical water creature
c) A flying horse

10 Which sport is especially popular in Wales?

a) Baseball
b) Cricket
c) Rugby

Label the Map

Label the countries, cities, islands, and bodies of water in the map below.

Flag Matching

Match the flag with the correct country.

England

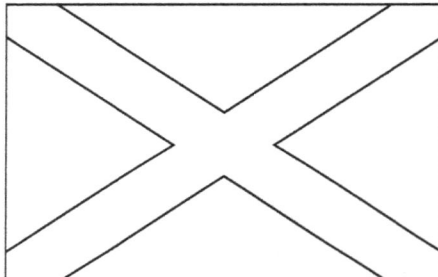

Scotland

Wales

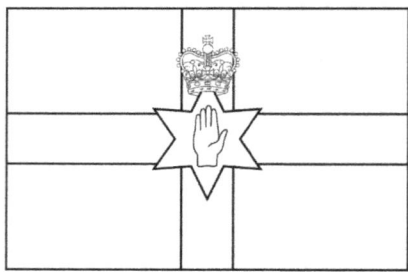

Northern Ireland

United Kingdom

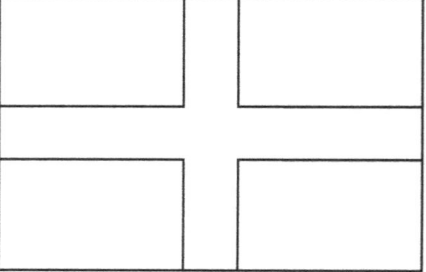

United Kingdom Crossword

Use what you've learned in this book to solve the puzzle.

Across

1. The UK's most famous clock tower (3,3)
5. Capital of England (6)
6. Traditional skirt worn in Scotland (4)
8. Highest mountain in the UK (3,5)
11. Traditional Scottish dish (6)
13. Warm drink popular in the UK (3)
14. Scottish musical instrument (8)
16. Country with the capital of Cardiff (5)
18. The red symbol on Wales' flag (6)
19. Scotland's national animal (7)

Down

2. Northern Ireland's capital (7)
3. England's national flower (4)
4. Capital of Scotland (9)
7. Popular game in Wales (5)
9. British author Hamlet and Macbeth (11)
10. Famous river running through London (6)
12. Name of the UK flag (5,4)
15. Type of patterned cloth worn in Scotland (6)
17. This word means "lake" in Scotland (4)

Answers

Mini Quiz Answers

1. Four
2. Edinburgh
3. False
4. Irish Sea
5. Blue, Red, White

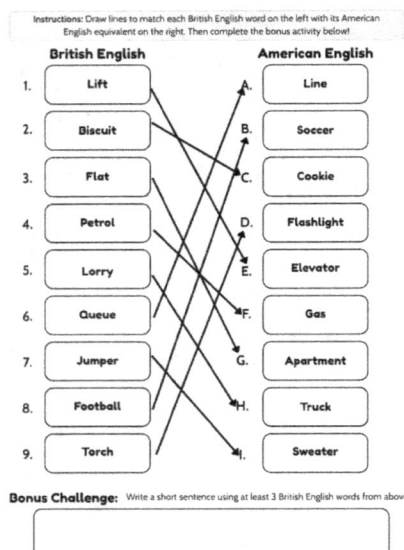

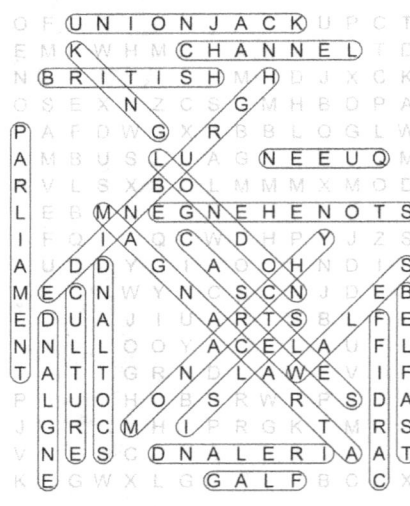

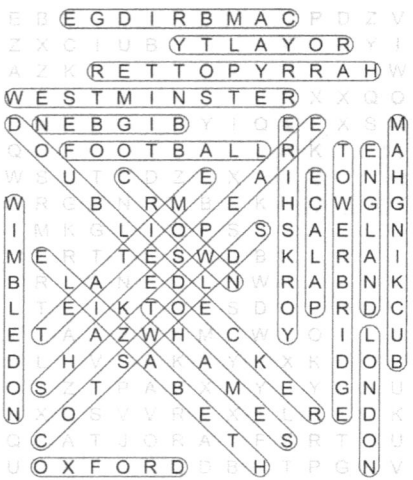

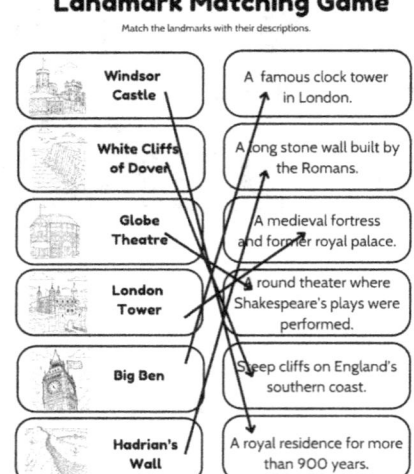

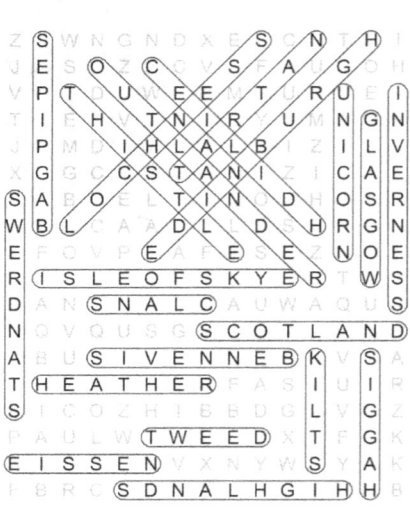

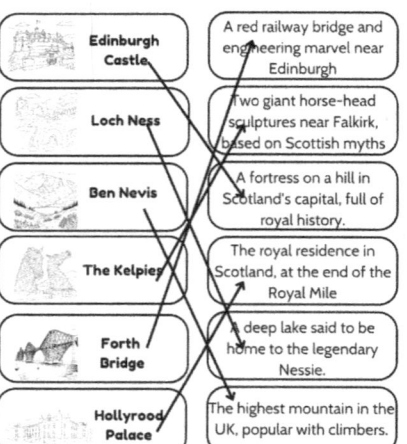

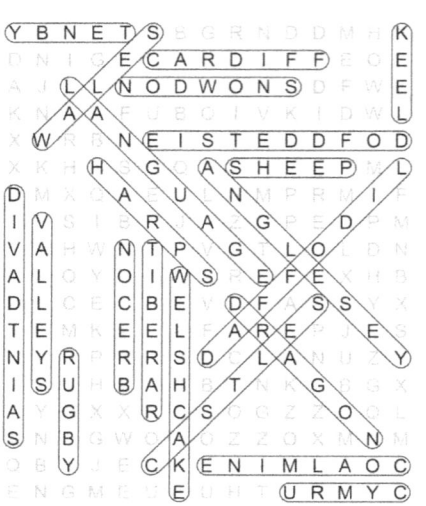

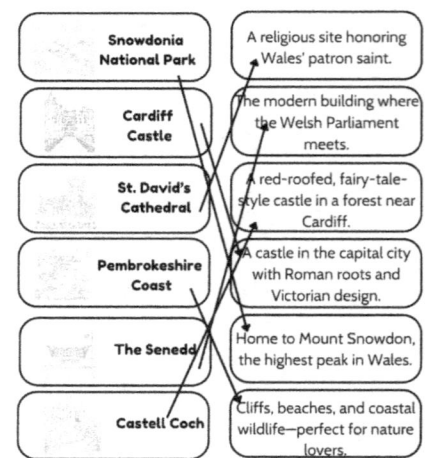

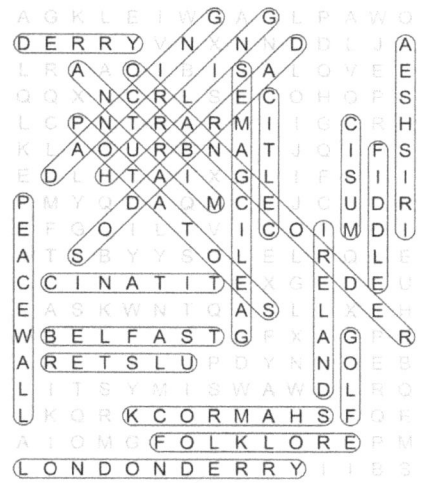

Landmark Matching Game
Match the landmarks with their descriptions.

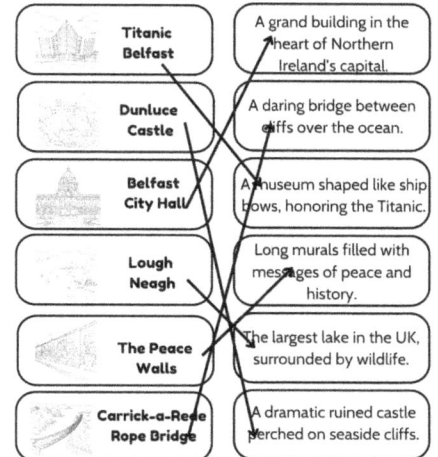

UK Quiz
Test your knowledge about the United Kingdom. Circle the correct answer.

1. What is the capital of Scotland?
   a) London
   b) Belfast
   c) Edinburgh

2. Which country is famous for the red dragon on its flag?
   a) Wales
   b) Ireland
   c) England

3. Where can you visit the Giant's Causeway?
   a) Wales
   b) Northern Ireland
   c) Scotland

4. What food is haggis most associated with?
   a) Wales
   b) England
   c) Scotland

5. Which UK country celebrates Guy Fawkes Night with fireworks?
   a) England
   b) Scotland
   c) Northern Ireland

6. What is the national flower of Wales?
   a) Thistle
   b) Daffodil
   c) Rose

7. Which famous clock tower stands in London?
   a) Big Ben
   b) Ben Nevis
   c) The Shard

8. Which UK country's patron saint is Saint Patrick?
   a) Scotland
   b) Northern Ireland
   c) Wales

9. What kind of animal is Nessie, the Loch Ness Monster?
   a) A giant cat
   b) A mythical water creature
   c) A flying horse

10. Which sport is especially popular in Wales?
    a) Baseball
    b) Cricket
    c) Rugby

Flag Matching
Match the flag with the correct country.

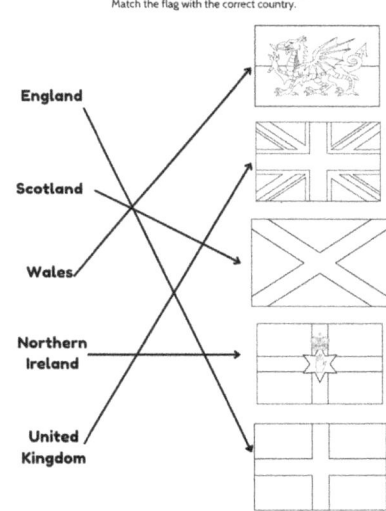